THE FALL

By Ryan Cahill

The Bound and The Broken

The Fall

Of Blood and Fire

THE FALL

THE BOUND AND THE BROKEN
NOVELLA

RYAN CAHILL

THE FALL

THE BOUND AND THE BROKEN NOVELLA

Copyright © Ryan Cahill 2021

First edition: May 2021

The right of RYAN CAHILL to be identified as the author of this work has been asserted by him in accordance with the Copyright, Designs and Patents Act 1988

ISBN 978-1-8383818-2-0

Published by Ryan Cahill

www.ryancahillauthor.com

To everyone who was told not to follow your dreams – do it anyway.

THE ARCHON

City of Ilnaen – Winter Solstice, Year 2682 after Doom

Alvira stood at the large, arched window, looking out over the central courtyard and onwards toward the sweeping walls of Ilnaen. Curtains of rain fell from dark thunderclouds. The reddish-pink light of the Blood Moon washed over the city of white stone, painting it in an eerie blend of beautiful and unsettling.

But it wasn't the Blood Moon that formed the knot in her stomach. She saw the torches in the distance, thousands of flickering flames, as if the plains themselves were on fire.

She reached out to Vyldrar. *Meet me at the council chamber.* Alvira felt a rumble of acknowledgement in the back of her mind. She strode across the room, snatched her sword from her bed, and buckled it to her hip. Then she stepped out into the hallway that ran adjacent to her bedchambers.

As Alvira emerged into the hallway, two elves charged at her, one in the shimmering red and gold uniform of the city guard, the other in the black robes of The Order's Battlemages, their swords drawn, fury etched on their smooth faces. A touch of panic threatened her mind, but she pushed it aside. She had no time for it. Ripping her sword free from its scabbard, she dipped under the first strike, then deflected the second, the ringing sound of steel-on-steel reverberating in her ears as the swords collided. A roaring pain burned through her side as the second elf raked his sword across her ribs, slicing a deep gash. She cursed herself for the decision to leave her plate armour with her handmaid.

Alvira reached out to the Spark. She saw it in her mind, its pulsating strands of twisting light interwoven together in the shape of a floating sphere. Each strand brimmed with the power of its element. Earth, Fire, Air, Water, and Spirit. Alvira pulled at the strand of Air, drawing threads of it into herself.

She swung her blade to parry the incoming strike from the elf to her right, then pulled at her threads of Air, using them to slam her second attacker into the white stone wall. She felt the resistance as the elf collided with the stone, and she heard the crunch as his bones gave way.

Spinning on her heels, Alvira lunged at her remaining attacker, deflecting his haphazard attempt to block her. She held her sword, outstretched, against his exposed neck.

"Who sent you?" Alvira roared, pushing her sword into his soft flesh.

The elf didn't answer. He just stared at her. His eyes were sunken and dark, and his skin was so pale that Alvira would have thought him close to death were he not standing before her. "Answer me!"

The elf ignored her and instead muttered something incoherent, resting his hand across his breastplate. As he did, a shimmering red glow emanated from beneath the steel plate. *Blood magic.* Alvira thrust her blade forward, plunging the tip into the elf's neck, attempting to stop him before he could tap into the power of the gemstone she knew hid beneath his armour. Blood cascaded from the wound as the elf hung there, held upright only by the strength of Alvira's arm. Stilling the knot in her gut, she pulled her blade free from the elf's neck and let him fall to the ground, spluttering and choking on his own blood.

With a deafening howl, a blinding eruption of deep red fire consumed the elf. The force of the blast knocked Alvira off her feet and sent her crashing into the wall behind her. A sharp pain pierced through her back and head as she hit the stone.

Groaning, she coughed out stone dust from her lungs and pulled herself up onto one knee. Her neck cracked as she rolled it side to side, a ringing noise droned through her head, and a blurry haze covered her eyes.

Blood magic was not detectable in the way that magic from the Spark was. It never triggered the tingling sensation she always experienced in the back of her mind when somebody near her drew from the Spark. Had she not seen the glow of the gemstone, it would have been her charred corpse that adorned the hallway floor.

Gritting her teeth, Alvira dragged herself to a standing position, using a nearby door frame for leverage. The gash in her side burned like a hot iron. *I need to get to the council. I need to find out what is happening.* She stumbled as she made her way down the sparse stone hallway, but she forced herself to keep moving, the muscles in her jaw twitching. Like most in that section of the keep, the floors and walls of the hallway were made from white flagstone, a deep crimson carpet running the length of the floor.

Alvira winced as she descended the staircase to the lower level. She felt the blood trickling down her ribcage with every step. She had been caught off guard. It would not happen again. She tightened the grip on her sword until her knuckles went pale.

The stone floor vibrated as the horns of the city watch bellowed through the hallway. She needed to find out what was happening. Who was attacking?

"Archon!" Alvira snapped her head to the right. Torvill, one of The Order's Highguard, stood at the end of a short corridor, waving Alvira to run to him. "Quick! We need to—" an arrow cut off Torvill's shout as it sliced through the side of his neck.

"It's the Archon! Kill her!"

Four men in half-plate armour rounded the corner where Torvill's lifeless body now lay in a pool of his own blood. Each of the men bore the joint symbol of The Order and the Draleid on their chests: a black triangle, pointing upward, with three smaller triangles set at each of its edges. These men were meant to be protecting her, not attacking her. A deep fury bubbled in Alvira's chest and her blood shivered through her veins, the rushing of it in her head causing all other sounds to capitulate. *Traitors.*

She drew on threads of Earth as the men charged down the hall towards her, heaving their weapons over their heads, screaming battle cries as they ran.

"You sicken me…" Alvira muttered, a snarl forming in her throat as she pulled the threads into her, feeling the rough grate at the back of her mind that came with drawing on Earth. She let out a blood-curdling roar as she held her hand out in front of herself, clenching her fingers into a tight fist. All four of the soldiers' breastplates collapsed inward, cracking their ribs and crushing their lungs. They fell to the ground with screams of agony, spluttering blood as they gasped for air. Alvira felt a momentary pang of sympathy as she stepped past the wailing wretches, which she quickly brushed aside.

They are traitors who would have my head on a spike.

Alvira's heart pounded. She rushed through the labyrinth of corridors that weaved through the keep of Ilnaen. They weren't just under attack – they had been betrayed. She needed to get to the council chamber; they weren't far now.

She drew on threads of Fire as she turned down the stone corridor to her left. Two soldiers were sprinting towards her. Both wore the glistening white armour of the Highguard, the symbol of The Order emblazoned across their chests, but their helms obscured their faces. Alvira did not let go of the Spark.

"Don't move any closer!" she shouted.

"Alvira, it's me." Alvira knew the elf's voice even before she removed her helmet.

"Valyna. By the gods, am I happy to see you." The ball of tension in Alvira's stomach dissipated as relief overcame her. She even allowed herself a weak smile as she set eyes on her friend. "What is going on?"

Valyna's mouth drew into a thin line. "The Uraks have breached the walls and surrounded the city. The city is split. I'm not sure how it started, but we stepped out into the training yard, and the men were slaughtering each other. We have been betrayed, Alvira."

"That much, I know. Have you seen Eltoar?"

"No, Archon."

"Farda?" An uneasy silence hung in the air. Only the muffled sounds of the battle drifted through the stone corridor. "Valyna, have you seen Farda?"

"Yes, Archon."

"Valyna… *Where* is Farda? We don't have time to stand around."

"He no longer fights for The Order, Alvira."

"What are you talking about? He—"

"The last we saw of him, he was riding astride Shinyara… setting the western wall aflame."

A shiver ran through Alvira's body.

Even Draleid have turned…

"How… How many, Valyna? How many Draleid have betrayed us?"

"I do not know, Archon. But the skies are on fire."

The Highguard who stood beside Valyna let out a sigh. "The gods have abandoned us, Archon. We should leave while we can. We need to get you and Vyldrar to safety," he said in a thick Drifaienin accent.

Alvira moved like lightning, clearing the space between herself and the man in the blink of an eye. She wrapped her fingers around the shimmering chainmail that covered the exposed area of his neck, between his helm and his breastplate. Clenching her hands tight around the mail, she drew his face level with her own, pulling on threads of Spirit, weaving them into her voice as she spoke, easing the man's fear.

"The gods have not abandoned us, just as we will not abandon the people we swore to protect. If we die tonight, we die with our swords in our hands, staring into the eyes of the one who sends us into the void. Do you hear me?"

Alvira stepped back. Her heart thumped in her chest as she released her grip on the man's chain mail. She had clenched it so hard that her knuckles had whitened and her fingers were stiff.

"Yes, Archon," the man said. His breaths were shallow, and there was regret in his voice.

Good. Be ashamed. Let it fuel your anger.

"Have you seen any of the council?" Alvira asked, turning to Valyna, who shook her head. "Okay, we need to get to the council chamber. We need to find out what is going on. Then we can organise the defence. Vyldrar will meet us there."

"Yes, Archon," Valyna said, nodding towards the man who was with her.

Alvira drew in a deep breath as they reached the top of the enormous staircase. The doors to the walkway stood in front of them, framed by thick walls of white stone. They were built from multiple layers of solid oak, reinforced with steel, and ornamented with gold plating. Anywhere else in Epheria, they would be considered art. But in Ilnaen, such works of beauty were commonplace.

"Archon… before we go out there…"

"We will have time for goodbyes later, Valyna. I don't plan on dying today." Alvira didn't wait for Valyna to respond. She turned, reaching for the Spark. She drew on thick threads of Air and slammed them into the heavy, reinforced doors, swinging them open with ease.

Dark thunderclouds pummelled rain down onto the stone surface of the walkway as Alvira stepped through the doors. The massive structure was nearly two hundred feet long and stood even higher off the ground.

The council chamber was nestled at the top of the city's tallest tower, the Tower of Faith, and the walkway bridged the chamber and the keep. Stepping out onto the bridge was like standing at the edge of a bottomless chasm.

Alvira fought back her fear and desolation as she looked out over the city that had been her home for over a hundred years. Valyna had not lied. The skies were on fire. Everywhere she looked, torrents of flame streaked across the sky. Rivers of dragonfire illuminated the depths of the heavy, charcoal-black clouds. The flowing rivers of flame only parted when they whirled around the scales of another dragon, like waves breaking on the bow of a ship. A small piece of her heart broke as she watched her brothers and sisters of the Draleid tear each other from the skies. This was not how it was meant to be.

Alvira jumped as a bolt of lightning shot down from the sky, crashing into the side of the tower. Chunks of stone whirled through the air, plummeting to the ground below. The city burned just as the skies did. The acrid smell of charred flesh and singed wood filled the air. Battle cries and wails of agony echoed throughout the streets of white stone.

Alvira reached out to Vyldrar again. He was close. *Be careful.*

"Valyna?" Alvira turned towards the Highguard, a questioning look on her face. *Will you go with me, follow me into the flames of our home?*

"We are with you, Archon."

"Until the end," added the man by her side, a boldness in his voice where before there had been none.

That's more like it. Alvira nodded and set off across the walkway.

Several shapes came into view about fifty feet ahead. Through the deluge, Alvira made out six figures. Five of them towered over the sixth, who moved in a whir of steel. The light from the dragonfire above caused the soldier's twin blades to shimmer. Alvira knew the hulking shapes to be Uraks. They were foul creatures, powerful, with leathery skin and eyes as red as blood. Creatures of the traitor god.

As Alvira and her companions drew closer, two of the Uraks now lay crumpled in a heap on the ground, and one moved with a debilitating limp. A shiver tickled the back of her mind as arcs of lightning shot from the tips of the man's blades. Howls resounded in the night as the man's three attackers plummeted to the city below.

Alvira and the Highguard approached. Rain hammered down over the man as he stood there, soaked to the bone, his black hair matted to his forehead. He sheathed his swords in the scabbards across his back as Alvira drew closer.

"Archon," he said, dropping to one knee and drawing a closed fist across his chest.

"Get off your knee, Aeson. This is no time for formality."

Aeson rose to his full height. He was a handsome man, with broad shoulders and an athletic build. His chest heaved with exertion, droplets of water dripping from his hair and nose. A fresh cut ran the length of his cheek, and blood trickled down the breast of his studded black leather armour, flowing from a deep gash along his left shoulder. Yet despite everything, his ice-blue eyes held a defiant stare. "Yes, Archon."

"Why are you here? Should you not be down there, in the city?"

"The First Sword tasked me with protecting the walkway. To stop all who attempted to enter the council chamber."

"Eltoar. He is in there?"

"Yes, Archon. He and the rest of the council."

"Are you going to try to stop *me* from entering?"

The young man smiled. For a moment, Alvira feared his answer. She knew his capabilities well. She was not sure she could best him in either the sword or the Spark.

"You are my Archon. My blades belong to you."

"*Draleid n'aldryr*," Alvira said, drawing a closed fist across her chest.

"*Draleid n'aldryr*," the man repeated, mimicking Alvira's gesture.

Alvira couldn't help the flicker of a smile that crept onto her face. "Aeson, I need you and the Highguard to stay here. Do as you have done. Nothing crosses this walkway. Understood?"

Aeson nodded, drawing his swords once again.

"Archon—"

Alvira cut Valyna off with a stern look.

"As you command, Archon."

The wind and the rain buffeted Alvira as her feet pounded the stone. Cracks of lightning and torrents of dragonfire illuminated the night sky. It was impossible to distinguish between the claps of thunder and the roar of the dragons overhead, such was the ferocity of the incredible creatures. A rumble in the back of her mind let her know that Vyldrar was perched on the roof, at the opposite side of the council chamber.

Only if needed.

The domed roof of the council chamber was built from solid gold. Large white banners hung in front of the great oak doors; the symbol of The Order emblazoned across them in black. It was a sight to behold. Many travelled the length and breadth of Epheria just to see it up close, but Alvira didn't have the time to admire its beauty.

No guards were stationed at the chamber doors. Eltoar obviously had faith in young Aeson.

Your faith is well-placed, old friend.

Alvira reached out to the Spark and heaved the giant doors open with threads of Air. She felt a slight sap of energy as she bounded into the chamber. The drain – the force that sapped her strength as she drew from the Spark – didn't affect her like it used to, but it was still there. Still lingering, leeching at her slowly. Waiting for the day that she drew too heavily, waiting to consume her soul.

Alvira ran her hands up over her face, wiping away the rainfall that clung to her skin. Water dripped from her hair and her leathers, forming a trail along the white stone floor as she walked.

The council chamber was as breathtaking on the inside as it was from the outside. The Order had commissioned the finest craftsmages for its construction. The floor of the central atrium consisted of interlaced gold and white stone, with the symbol of the Order at its centre, in jet-black. The central atrium was ringed by a colonnade of ornate, forty-foot-high columns of white stone. Enormous black and white banners draped the front of every second column. Interspersed between the columns stood six massive statues. Standing over twenty feet tall, each statue represented one of the six gods.

Varyn, The Father, stood directly across from the main entrance. The Mother, Heraya, was at his side. Both wore long, flowing robes, with circlets atop their heads. Alvira could not think of a way that the craftsmages could have made them look more noble.

Halfway across the chamber, facing each other from opposite sides, stood Elyara and Achyron, The Maiden and The Warrior. The two statues closest to the entrance depicted Hafaesir and Neron, The Smith and The Sailor.

There was no statue for Efialtír, the traitor god.

Hundreds of candles in sconces all about the chamber illuminated the golden dome with an incandescent glow, though the candlelight did not burn as brightly as usual. The chamber seemed shrouded in a dimness, as though the light itself retreated from the shadow.

"Eltoar!" Alvira's call echoed through the empty chamber as the candles made shadows dance across the floor. The only response was the muffled drum of rain, interspersed with claps of thunder, as it battered the dome, drowning out the fighting in the city streets. Alvira walked out into the centre of the massive chamber, stopping atop the black stone symbol of The Order.

Footsteps sounded through the chamber. "Alvira. You're alive."

Eltoar Daethana was the First Sword of the Draleid, Alvira's second in command, and her oldest friend. His snow-white hair coruscated in the dim candlelight as he stepped from behind the colonnade. The colour of his full plate armour matched it, with an ostentatious trim of gold and the symbol of The Order emblazoned across its front. His face was sharp and angular, and his ears tapered off into a point, like all elves'.

"I am, thank the gods. It is good to find you. Where are the rest of the council?"

Alvira thought she saw the corners of Eltoar's mouth twist into a frown, a touch of sadness in his eyes. It was hard to tell at that distance and in the dim light. He did not answer. He stared at her as he circled the edge of the colonnade, his slow and purposeful steps echoing off the stone. *Something is wrong.*

"Eltoar. Where are the rest of the council?"

"Always worried," Eltoar said, shaking his head. "Always worried about the damned council. All they have ever done, Alvira, is hold us back. You know it to be true."

Alvira tightened her grip on the handle of her sword. "Eltoar… what are you saying—" Something wet and cold dripped onto Alvira's cheek. Rain still drummed against the outside of the dome. Perhaps the lightning or the battle had cracked its surface. Alvira wiped away the droplet, but when she brought her hand away from her face, crimson blood smeared her fingertips.

She looked up at the dome. She had only given it a passing glance when she entered. Her eyes narrowed as she attempted to understand what she was seeing. A chill ran through her as the light settled on the disfigured shapes that hung in the air, close to the surface of the dome. *The council.*

She couldn't feel Eltoar drawing from the Spark, yet the bodies hung in the air. A knot twisted in her stomach and a shiver ran the length of her spine. She looked at Eltoar, who now stood before her. "Eltoar, what have you done?"

"I have done what needed to be done, Alvira. I have freed us, given us the power to forge our own path."

"Eltoar… no…"

Eltoar's face twisted into a snarl. Dark circles hung under his eyes, as though he hadn't slept in weeks. "What? You would have us sit under the council's thumb for eternity? We are *Draleid*, Alvira. When Fane told me his plans—"

"Fane?" Alvira spat. "That twisted mage? Eltoar, you know better than most what he is capable of. Open your eyes! Look at what you have done. The city reeks of blood magic!"

"You speak of what you do not understand," Eltoar hissed. "I did what I had to do. It was the only way…"

"Eltoar, our friends are dying out there! The council… How… I knew you were unhappy with things, but Eltoar, how could you do this?"

"It didn't have to be this way…" Eltoar said, a melancholy clinging to his words. Alvira could see the hesitation in Eltoar's eyes, his mind snapping back and forth between anger and grief. "You should have listened to me long ago…" Eltoar's expression hardened, his eyes turning to a cold stare. "But it is too late now. Sacrifices must be made so that we can be reborn, Alvira. Efialtír demands it."

"Efialtír? The *traitor god*? Eltoar, have you lost your mind?"

"He sees the way," said a raspy voice from over Alvira's shoulder.

"The one true god," answered a second voice.

Two hooded figures emerged from the shadows of the colonnade behind Alvira, their black cloaks drinking in the weak candlelight.

"Eltoar? Is this how far you are willing to go? Would you see my blood stain this floor?"

"You know I do not want it that way," Eltoar said, holding his hands out wide. "Join me, Alvira. Help me build a new world where the Draleid are not beholden to the whims of a corrupt council who line their pockets with the gold of kings. The Draleid are more than this. *You* are more than this. You are our Archon." Eltoar paused for a moment, a longing in his eyes. "Please…"

"This is not the way! I would rather burn for eternity than betray our brothers and sisters."

"That can be arranged," one of the men behind Alvira hissed.

Alvira ignored him and focused on Eltoar. "Eltoar… tell me you didn't do that." She looked up at the eight mutilated bodies that hung in the air along the surface of the dome. "Tell me… For the love of the gods…"

"Sacrifices *must* be made, Alvira."

Alvira felt her heart bleed as the words left Eltoar's lips. She stared into his cold eyes. The man she knew was still there, he had to be. "Eltoar… no."

Eltoar's lip curled in resignation. "So be it," he said, a reluctant sigh accompanying his words. He gave a slight nod to the men behind her.

Alvira spun on her heels, drawing on threads of Spirit and Fire. She didn't feel the hooded man reach for the Spark, but arcs of purple lightning erupted from his outstretched hand. Alvira met the lightning with Spirit and Fire, redirecting it towards the second man. The force of the lightning lifted him off his feet, shards of shattered stone flying in all directions as it cracked into the ground.

Alvira leapt towards the first man, swinging her blade in an arc. With inhuman speed, he drew his blade and caught Alvira's strike. But he wasn't fast enough to block the dagger she pulled from her hip before she drove it through his heart.

A low, rumbling laugh filled the chamber. A weightless feeling settled in Alvira's stomach and fear shivered through her as she realised the laughter came from the man with the dagger in his chest. She let go of the hilt, stumbling backwards, her heart pounding. "How?"

The man pulled the dagger from his flesh, letting it drop to the ground with a clang. He cracked his jaw from side to side, rolling his neck as though he were trying to relieve a stiff ache. But not a drop of blood seeped from the wound.

He pulled his hood back off his head and stepped towards Alvira. His skin was so pale it almost matched the white of the stone from which the city was built. He twisted his lips into an attenuated grin and stared at her with jet-black eyes.

A shiver ran down Alvira's spine when she realised what the creature was. *A Fade.* A mage that had opened himself to the traitor god and shared his body with dark spirits.

Alvira felt the Fade reach for the Spark, but she wasn't quick enough to react. Threads of Air slammed into her chest, catapulting her into the base of one of the columns. She softened the blow with a cushion of Air, but she still felt the pang of pain shoot up her spine. She landed on one knee, shaking as she rose to her feet. A sharp pain still burned along her ribs from her earlier wound, but she ignored it.

"This one has some fight," hissed a voice to her left. The other Fade, whom she had hit with the lightning, was now on his feet. He clutched a sword of black fire in his porcelain-pale fingers.

A níthral.

The two Fades closed in on her, circling like wolves. They drew so heavily from the Spark that Alvira felt it pulsating from their bodies. The drain did not seem to affect them, at least, not like it did her.

Eltoar didn't move to help her – or hurt her. He just stood there and watched. He had been her closest friend, the one person she thought she could trust implicitly. And now he just stood aside, happy to watch her die.

Alvira let her sword drop to the ground and reached out to the Spark. Fire, Earth, Water, Air, and Spirit. She drew from them all. It was necessary to form a níthral – a *Soulblade.*

She felt the thrum of the Spark pulsing through her. Tendrils of piercing blue light burst from her hand in both directions, twisting and turning around each other. As they moved, they left a solid form in their wake. It took only seconds for the form to take shape as Alvira stood in between the two Fades, her hands wrapped around the long haft of a double-bladed sword that glowed with blue light. It felt almost weightless in her hands. She took a deep breath. And then the Fades were upon her.

They slashed at her with their black-fire blades, snapping like vipers. The forms flowed through Alvira's mind. She moved into the *fellensír* – the Lonely Mountain. A defensive movement practised by warriors of The Order, for when they were outnumbered.

Her lungs heaved as the Fades battered at her defences. Alone, she might have been able to take them. They were skilled swordsmen. She was better. But the two of them together were too strong. They nipped at her with threads of Fire and Air, trying to catch her off guard. She held firm, but she was tiring.

She swung her *níthral* up, catching the downstroke of the Fade's sword in a burst of blue light. Immediately, she pivoted, swinging low across the ground and sweeping her blade upward.

A horrifying shriek resonated through the chamber as Alvira's glowing blue blade sheared straight through the Fade's arm. The creature wailed and snarled as it hunched back defensively. Still, Eltoar did not move. He simply observed.

Another thick thread of Air crashed into Alvira's chest. She caught herself before she collided with the wall of the chamber, but only just.

The two Fades closed in on her. They stood only a few feet apart, their black-fire blades seeming to draw in light as they blazed. Alvira stood up straight, took a deep breath, and set herself for what was to come.

The Fades charged.

A fierce wave of fear and anger flooded from Vyldrar's mind into Alvira's, accompanied by a monstrous roar that shook the very foundations of the chamber. Alvira did not keep the smile from spreading across her face as she wreathed herself in a bubble of Air.

The wall behind her exploded inward in a cloud of stone and dust. The Fades shielded their eyes as the rubble crashed down onto the atrium floor.

In the gaping hole where the wall behind her had once stood was the hulking figure of Vyldrar. Dark green scales covered his muscular body, shining like emeralds in the pale pinkish moonlight. Deep black pupils bisected his yellow eyes. Ridges of long horns framed his face, under his jaw and back up along his neck. The hole he had created was not nearly big enough for him to fit through, but his powerful forelimbs clung to the inside of the chamber. A more magnificent dragon she had never laid eyes on. Alvira felt Vyldrar's anger smouldering in her chest.

Fear painted the Fades' paper-thin faces. Even those dark creatures could not stand against dragonfire.

Vyldrar extended his thick, muscular neck over Alvira, a deep rumble emanating from his throat. The dragon's chest expanded as his massive, leathery wings spread and rose backwards. That familiar pressure built at the back of Alvira's consciousness. His mouth opened to expose a fearsome array of teeth, the smallest being the size of a dagger. Orange-red flames began to pour from his jaws. What began as a flicker became a river of incandescent dragonfire that lit the council chamber like a bonfire.

The Fades screamed as they burned. The sound was like nothing born of the natural world. Their piercing shrieks seemed to contain a multitude of voices that howled as they were ripped from the world.

The shrieking stopped before the dragonfire did. As Vyldrar's flames dissipated and flickered from existence, all that was left behind were a pair of charred, crumpled husks.

The dim bluish glow of Alvira's níthral washed over the white stone. Sweat dripped down her forehead, and blood seeped from the variegated wounds that laced her body.

With the gaping hole in the chamber's wall, the sound of hammering rainfall filled the atrium. The natural acoustics of the building made the claps of thunder sound like explosions in Alvira's ear. But amidst it all, Alvira heard the clink of steel boots against the stone floor.

"Join me," Eltoar said again. He stood over the charred corpses of the Fades. His white plate armour was pristine, unmarred by either dirt or blood. "We will create a world where we are not beholden to the whims of kings and queens. A world where *we* are the kings and queens."

Alvira felt Vyldrar scratching at the back of her mind. His anger burned as brightly as ever. She felt the pressure building again and heard the low rumble in his chest. "I will never betray The Order."

"The Order is gone!" Eltoar roared. "It is destroyed, and the council are dead. Their hypocrisy, their lies, and deceit. Dead! Do not be a fool. You can lead us into this new world, do not throw that away over misplaced loyalty."

Alvira stared at Eltoar, examining the man she once knew. A man that was no more. "What happened to you?"

"I opened my eyes Alvira. I saw what you still fail to see. You—"

"I will not join you, Eltoar." Alvira said, cutting Eltoar short. "I will not walk down that path."

"Damn you, Alvira!" Eltoar shouted, fury burning in his eyes. "So be it. Die with them. Die with your beloved Order!"

A bone-shattering roar erupted in the exposed skies overhead. Alvira's shoulders dropped and her spirit sank into the pit of her stomach. She could just make out the terrifyingly massive outline of Helios – the dragon to which Eltoar was bonded – soaring through the sky. The night sky, burning with dragonfire, all but obscured Helios's deep black and red scales. Were it not for the bolts of lightning that streaked through the thunderclouds, it would have been easy to mistake him for a trick of the eye.

The monstrous dragon crashed straight into Vyldrar. Its immense jaws closed around the neck of the smaller dragon. The force of the collision tore Vyldrar away from the side of the chamber. His talons gouged furrows in the stone as the two dragons spiralled down into the city below.

"Vyldrar!" Alvira screamed. She leapt over to the edge of the stone, where the opening in the wall gave way to the sky. Her heart wrenched in her chest as she watched the two immense figures crash down into the city streets, hundreds of feet below.

Alvira collapsed to her knees. She felt Vyldrar's pain. Helios was easily twice his size, and she felt every gash that the monstrous creature raked in Vyldrar's side. She felt the dragon's jaws clamp around Vyldrar's neck and his teeth tear away chunks of flesh. She felt his fear. He had always been her better half. He was strong when she was weak, and courageous when she cowered. But now *she* felt *his* fear.

Something in her body broke when she felt him die, like a pane of glass shattering into a million pieces. She went numb. It was said that when a Draleid or their dragon dies, the other becomes broken. Half of something that would never be whole again.

She felt the cold steel of Eltoar's sword nestle against the nape of her neck. She knelt in the rubble of the broken wall, tears rolling down her cheeks. She looked out over the city. Blazing infernos rose across its sweeping streets. Hundreds of dragons filled the eldritch skies above, their silhouettes illuminated by the cracks of lightning that tore through the sky.

"I never wanted it to come to this, Alvira," Eltoar said, a resignation in his voice.

Alvira didn't respond. She took one last look over the city.

Eltoar swung his blade.

Alvira closed her eyes.

THE KNIGHTS

C andles flickered, warming the cold stone walls of the enormous chamber – the heart of the great temple of Achyron.

Brother-Captain Kallinvar felt the thrum of his Sentinel armour resonating through him from the Sigil fused into his chest. Smooth, overlapping plates of dark green covered every inch of his body, as hard as any metal and as light as a whisper. It was not forged in a smithy by hammer and fire. No, it was called forth, wrought by Spirit. It was a gift bestowed upon the Knights of Achyron millennia ago by the warrior god himself. Kallinvar knew no greater comfort than that familiar thrum of power that resonated through him.

All around, he saw his brother and sister knights, encased in their armour. The Sigil of Achyron – a downward-facing sword set into a sunburst – was emblazoned across their chests in brilliant white, to match the cloaks that streamed behind them. It was a sight to behold.

"Listen to me, brothers and sisters." Grandmaster Verathin stood beside Kallinvar. The golden ornamentation of his Sentinel armour marked his rank. The man was the best of them. He had stood at their head for years beyond counting, and he was Kallinvar's closest friend. "I do not know what we will face on the other side. I do not know if we will survive. But a darkness has fallen over Ilnaen. I can feel it. We must go. We must hold back the shadow." Verathin turned to Kallinvar. "Do you wish to lead the way, Brother-Captain Kallinvar?"

It is time.

Kallinvar nodded. He pulled his sword from its sheath. The long steel blade shimmered in the incandescent candlelight.

"We stand when others cannot," Kallinvar roared. He beat the handle of his sword off his armoured chest, a drum of war. The sound of a hundred swords colliding with plated chests filled the chamber as the knights followed Kallinvar's lead. "We have been given a sacred duty. *We* were chosen! Achyron himself led the Grandmaster to each and every one of us. Men and women on the verge of death, who still had more to give to this world. The strength of The Warrior burns in our veins!"

The rhythmic hammering of steel on armour grew louder and louder, and Kallinvar's heart beat in unison.

"*This* is what we do. We stand against the darkest nights. When all hope is lost, we are the brightest light!" Kallinvar's chest swelled with pride as the knights crashed their swords against their armour, the sound consuming the chamber. He felt the fire of battle burning in his chest.

A familiar sensation tickled at the back of Kallinvar's neck. Verathin was opening the Rift.

"When we get to the other side," Kallinvar shouted, his voice booming, "remember what we fight for. Remember *who* we fight for. Are you with me, brothers and sisters?"

The deafening shouts of the knights echoed through the chamber.

The hairs on the back of his neck stood on end as a tiny green orb appeared, hanging in the air ten feet in front of him. The orb spread into a circle about two feet in diameter and kept growing. Its edges were a vivid lime-green, growing darker towards the centre, where it was almost black.

The war drum of swords on armour grew louder, blending with the chants and shouts. But to Kallinvar, all sounds capitulated to the thrum that resonated through his body as Verathin opened the Rift.

The Rift was another gift from Achyron, a gift only given to the Grandmaster. It gave him the power to travel anywhere in the known world in an instant. The circle continued to grow until it was over twenty feet in diameter. Its surface rippled with energy as everything but its outer rim, which still burned a bright green, faded to black.

Going through the Rift always gave Kallinvar an uneasy feeling in his stomach. It was what he imagined it would be like to enter the void.

Kallinvar took a deep breath, holding it to settle himself. Fear always came before the calm of battle. He turned to Verathin, who held his gaze for what seemed like an eternity before giving him a sombre nod.

"For Achyron!" Kallinvar roared.

"For Achyron!" came the reply. The war drum of one hundred swords picked up its pace until the chamber was a din of steel on steel. One hundred swords for one hundred knights, as it had always been.

One last deep breath and Kallinvar lunged forward, charging at the rippling lake of black that hung in the air. He did not know what lay in front of him. The Rift never allowed them to see. But he didn't need to look to know the rest of the knights were behind him – and that was what mattered.

Even through the Sentinel armour, Kallinvar felt the Rift's icy embrace wash over him as he plunged through its surface. Every hair on his body stood on end as the chill seeped from his skin to his bones. It was only a moment, and then he was through, into the training yard, in the western section of Ilnaen.

Everything before his eyes was chaos. Dark storm clouds emptied blankets of rain and rippled the air with claps of thunder. The incandescent glow of burning buildings mingled with the pale wash of pinkish-red light that drifted down from the Blood Moon to illuminate the city. The usually pristine, white stone buildings of Ilnaen were incarnadined with the blood of the fallen. All across the training yard, soldiers who should have been on the same side fought tooth and nail. Kallinvar watched as a Praetorian drove his sword through the back of an elderly woman whom he should have been protecting.

He felt the sickly Taint of blood magic seeping from the Praetorian long before he saw the pale, almost translucent skin of his face and the bloody holes where his eyes should have been. A shiver ran down his spine at the sight of the blood and torn flesh in the man's empty sockets.

What in the gods is happening here?

Kallinvar grunted as a hammer blow caught him in the side before he had time to set his feet. He stumbled, catching his heel on the white steel breastplate of a fallen soldier, one of The Order's Highguard.

A particularly large Urak wielded the hammer that had struck him. The monstrosity of a creature stood nearly a foot taller than Kallinvar. Its leathery skin was a mottled brownish-grey, and its body was laden with thick, heavy muscle. Black slits bisected its crimson eyes.

The fear in Kallinvar's mind was replaced by the calm of battle. He swivelled, dug his heel into the ground, and swung his arm through the air, catching the second swing of the hammer in mid-air. Only a slight vibration shook through his arm as the heavy weapon crashed into his open palm, the Sentinel armour absorbing most of the impact. A look of shock spread across the creature's face.

Before Kallinvar could move to strike the Urak, the hammer fell to the ground, the beast's leathery fingers still wrapped around its shaft. Grandmaster Verathin stepped between Kallinvar and the Urak, that now howled in pain over its severed arm, and plunged his sword through the beast's belly.

"Take your knights and find the Archon and the council. I suspect she will either be somewhere on the battlefield or at the council chamber. Best to start there. We will try to turn the tide here."

"Yes, Grandmaster. Knights of the Second, with me!"

The nine knights under Kallinvar's command fell in behind him as he carved his way through the training yard and out into the city beyond. The Sigil of Achyron that had been fused with his chest all those years ago granted him great strength. It seeped into his muscles and burned in his veins. It was a strength that was needed to fight the Bloodspawn, to stand toe-to-toe with creatures who were bred to kill.

Streaks of dragonfire tore through the skies overhead, illuminating the streets. Kallinvar and his knights fought their way across the city, towards the council chamber.

Every thoroughfare and side street they passed was wet with blood. Kallinvar sensed the Taint of blood magic all around him. All the knights could. It was like a sickly oil that seeped into the back of his mind, causing his consciousness to recoil. The city reeked of it.

Many of the soldiers within the city had been twisted and tainted by its dark touch. They were little more than vessels. But some of them had opened themselves to it, bathed in it of their own free will.

At the corner of one of the many courtyards they passed through, two mages ripped each other to shreds with their magic. The Spark. Kallinvar could not sense the Spark the way he could sense blood magic. Only those who could touch the Spark could sense it in others.

Each of the mages wore gleaming half-plate armour of white steel. Black cloaks billowed out behind them.

Battlemages of The Order.

They struck each other with bolts of lightning and slammed each other off buildings. Both survived blows they had no right to survive, but such was the power of the

Battlemages. They were famous across Epheria. Some were even a match to the Draleid in strength.

In a flash, one of the Battlemages whirred his sword through the air, decapitating a nearby soldier. Kallinvar felt the Taint pulsate in the heavy air as the Battlemage drew the man's Essence from his blood. Emboldened by the kill, the Battlemage turned back to face his counterpart. His hands outstretched, arcs of purple lightning streaked from his fingertips. The lightning ripped through the other Battlemage, burning holes straight through his body and shattering the stone wall behind him.

A sickly shiver ran down Kallinvar's spine as the surviving Battlemage turned. His eyes were as black as the darkest night, from corner to corner. His skin was as white as snow. Kallinvar knew what the creature was instantly.

"Fade," he hissed.

"The Taint touches every corner of this city," Ruon said, in her harsh Valtaran accent. "I want that creature dead as much as you do, Brother-Captain, but we need to keep moving."

"Aye," Ildris said. "Ruon is right, loathe as I am to admit it."

Kallinvar could not see Ruon's face, but he knew she was smiling beneath her helm. *She's always smiling. Or grinning more like.*

Kallinvar took one more glance back at the Fade. The creature was gone, and it had left more than one body in its wake. "Okay, keep moving."

As they made their way through a side street behind the keep, Ildris stopped dead in his tracks, throwing a glance towards Kallinvar.

Kallinvar felt it too: a sudden rush of the Taint. It seeped into his mind, sending shivers down the length of his back.

Bloodmarked.

Almost as soon as the feeling touched the back of his mind, an enormous creature crashed through the wall of the side street, about twenty feet ahead. Fragments of stone soared through the air, crushing soldiers and Uraks alike, filling the street with clouds of dust.

The Bloodmarked were Uraks. At least, they used to be. The monstrosity that stood before them was at least ten feet tall. Its body was so heavily laden with muscle that it looked as though its leathery skin might tear open at any moment. But its size was not what set it apart from the other Uraks. Smoke drifted from sets of glowing red runes that covered its chest, back, and arms.

Blood runes. Markings of ancient magic carved straight into the beast's flesh by the hand of a shaman. Kallinvar did not know much about blood runes. None of the knights did. Over the centuries, they had tried to learn as much as they could, and the priests chronicled their findings. Despite their efforts, that section of the great library remained sparse. Unsurprisingly, Urak shamans were never willing to give up any information.

All Kallinvar knew was that the Bloodmarked were vicious monstrosities that destroyed everything in their path.

"So," Kallinvar said, turning to Ruon, "seeing as *this* one is blocking our path…"

Ruon sighed, which only made Kallinvar laugh.

"Get some of these soldiers to safety. The duty of the strong is to protect the weak."

"The duty of the strong is to protect the weak," Ruon repeated. "Knights of the Second, spread out. Get the soldiers to safety. Kill any who bear the Taint."

As the nine other knights moved about the wide street, Kallinvar sheathed his sword. It would be no use against a Bloodmarked. He felt the strength of the Sentinel armour surging through him as he charged at the beast. Its smooth, overlapping plates did not hinder his movement like regular plate armour would have. When he wore the Sentinel armour, Kallinvar felt as though he could tear through a mountain and leave behind nothing but dust.

Ahead of him, the creature slammed its fist onto a fallen soldier, crushing the man's breastplate instantly. Rising to its full height, the beast settled its blood-red eyes on Kallinvar, who dashed towards it at full speed.

The Taint of blood magic oozed from the creature. It slammed its fist into the ground again, sending a shockwave of fire and stone hurtling towards Kallinvar.

Kallinvar bent at the knees, dug the balls of his feet into the ground, and launched himself over the shockwave, straight towards his target. He hung in the air for what felt like an eternity before crashing into the creature's chest with such force that it knocked the wind from his lungs. Both Kallinvar and the Bloodmarked crashed through the wall of a nearby building.

Kallinvar's head spun and his lungs dragged in stone dust as he gasped for air. But he did not have time to waste. He heaved himself up onto his knees, feeling the hard flesh of the Bloodmarked beneath him.

The creature snarled, its red eyes glowing with rage. Kallinvar threw his arm back and rammed his gauntleted fist into its face. He felt the crunch of bone meet the metal of his Sentinel armour, but the beast barely flinched. Kallinvar hit it again. A punch like that by someone wearing Sentinel armour would have killed a man instantly, but all the damage Kallinvar could see were a few flecks of blood on the beast's jagged, yellow teeth.

Kallinvar felt something large wrap around his ankle.

Fuck.

The beast's fingers tightened, lifted him, and flung him through the air. He collided with something solid, and a ringing noise filled his head. He dragged himself to his feet, using whatever he had collided with as leverage. Looking down, Kallinvar saw his hand resting on an enormous wrought iron anvil that now had a sizable dent in its side. The building they crashed into must have been a forge. *Well, that explains why my ribs hurt.*

A visceral roar filled the half-wrecked forge as the creature charged at Kallinvar. The deep red glow from its blood runes cast a shimmering light through the clouds of dust.

I need to end this. We don't have time.

Kallinvar emptied his mind, focusing on nothing but the Sigil that lay under his Sentinel armour, marked into his chest. A gift and a burden given to every knight. He felt its power coursing through his veins. A low, resounding thump. A heartbeat. *His* heartbeat.

Feeling the power of the Sigil, Kallinvar summoned his Soulblade. He felt the Spirit burning in his hand. Strands of green light burst from his fist in both directions, wrapping around each other, twisting and turning, leaving behind a solid shape in their wake. Within fractions of a second, the entire weapon was corporeal.

He held a massive greatsword of glowing green light, wrought from the spirit of Achyron. It was the weapon of the knighthood: the Soulblade. Some mages or Draleid who were powerful enough could imitate it. But that is what their níthrals were: poor imitations. They did not understand the power of a *true* Soulblade, wrought from the spirit of Achyron himself.

The beast was within arm's reach, charging with its head down. Kallinvar lunged to meet it. Just as they were about to collide, Kallinvar dropped to the ground, sliding beneath the monstrous creature.

The Bloodmarked was powerful and swift, but the blood runes clouded its mind. It was not quick to react.

With a swing of his Soulblade, he sheared straight through the beast's leg, splitting it in two at the knee. It howled in pain. Kallinvar did not pause. He bolted to his feet. Digging his foot into the ground, he launched himself. Swinging his Soulblade again, he separated the beast's arm from its shoulder. The Soulblade cut through its thick hide and dense bone as if they were paper.

The beast howled as it crashed to the ground, its blood runes burning with red light. Blood runes always burned brighter when the Bloodmarked were injured or dying. The priests believed the runes were attempting to keep their host alive. Kallinvar was inclined to agree.

He stood over the maimed creature as it howled and thrashed. Not even the slightest feeling of sympathy crossed his mind as he drove his Soulblade through its chest, where its heart should have been. Its blood runes burned with an intense fury; smoke streamed from the deep markings carved into its flesh. The red light mingled

33

with the green glow of Kallinvar's Soulblade as he twisted it deeper into the beast's chest. The creature roared, spraying blood and bits of flesh into the air. Its breath smelled of death and burning coals. Kallinvar stood over it until the glow from the blood runes dissipated and the creature lay still.

"Brother-Captain." Ildris approached Kallinvar, blood splattered across his helm. "The street is clear. Are we to keep moving?"

"Yes," Kallinvar replied, releasing his Soulblade. His body felt almost empty without the constant flow of Spirit burning through him. The absence of it seemed to dull his senses, just for a moment. "With every passing minute, the city comes closer to ruin."

"I fear it is already there, Brother-Captain."

Beneath his helm, Kallinvar's mouth was a grim line. His heart held heavy as he looked out through the destroyed wall of the forge, onward to the dark night sky streaked with plumes of dragonfire. They had come too late, waited far too long. *I fear it is too, brother.*

With one last look at the grotesque creature that lay lifeless in the rubble, Kallinvar stepped out from the ruined forge and back into the street. The rest of the knights stood waiting for him, Ruon at their head. "We continue on and make for the council chamber."

"Yes, Brother-Captain," the knights chorused.

Kallinvar had fought beside many of them since he first received the Sigil, nearly three centuries ago. They were his brothers and sisters in more than just name. However, in those three centuries, he had felt nothing like the fear he felt now. He had never felt the Taint so strongly. It hung in the air and seeped into the ground. *This battle is about more than just the fate of Ilnaen or The Order.* Kallinvar pushed his thoughts to the back of his mind. They would not help him.

It did not take long for them to reach a side entrance to the keep. Atop a small staircase, a set of reinforced doors were set into the side of the massive structure. Kallinvar had only been inside Ilnaen three times before, but his memory was clear. He knew that once they went through those doors, it would only be a few minutes before they reached the walkway that bridged the keep and the council chamber.

An ear-splitting roar filled the night as the knights scaled the staircase. For a few moments, the street was bathed in darkness as an enormous figure flew low over the city. A flicker of hesitation passed through Kallinvar's mind. He had not entertained the idea that some of the Draleid might have succumbed to the darkness. The very notion of it filled him with dread. He saw the same hesitation on Ildris's face. "We keep moving."

Ildris gave a brief nod before pushing open the doors.

The long, cold hallways of the keep did not hold much of note. They were built from the same white stone as the rest of the city. A red carpet ran along the length of every corridor. The combination of colours reminded Kallinvar of death. The cold, pale transparency of a dead man's skin mixed with the blood that he had lost.

The Order decorated sparsely, but the ornamentation they chose always displayed their vast wealth. The sconces that lined the walls were cast from solid gold. The candles themselves emitted the fragrant aroma of flowers, but not any that Kallinvar recognised. They were exotic flowers, the likes of which were sold in Vaerleon for fists full of silver by the traders that crossed the Narvonan Sea.

Except for the odd servant or housemaid in red and gold livery fleeing in panic, the hallways of the keep were empty. At least, they were empty of the living. Bodies lay everywhere, strewn about the floor like spilt grain. Men, women, elves, Jotnar, even children. Their wounds were gruesome. Some were split from head to groin. Some were missing limbs. Others were barely recognisable. Even to someone like Kallinvar, who had seen death in more forms than most, the scene made the hairs on his neck stand up and set an uneasy feeling in his stomach. The killing was senseless and twisted. *This is not a siege. It is an eradication.*

Before long, the knights reached the enormous staircase that led to the walkway. The doors that stood in front of them, framed by thick walls of white stone, were another example of the ostentatious taste of the people who had built Ilnaen. Practicality hidden behind beauty. Kallinvar could think of quite a few different ways he would have spent the gold paid to construct those doors.

He stepped past Ildris – the first to reach the top of the staircase – and pushed open the two doors. His Sentinel armour made them seem as light as paper.

The keep provided a brief respite from the din of battle that roared throughout the city, if not from the death and destruction that the Bloodspawn had left in their wake. But as soon as Kallinvar stepped out onto the walkway, everything came flooding back.

The dark thunderclouds that filled the sky were illuminated by a grimly beautiful blend of pinkish-red light from the Blood

Moon, the blaze of dragonfire, and blinding flashes of lightning. The rain drummed on Kallinvar's armour as he stared up at the sky. He heard it and saw it, but he did not feel it; the Sentinel armour left no gaps.

A brief nod to Ildris and Ruon, and they all started across the gargantuan stone bridge. There was no second of command in the knight chapters, not officially. There was only the Captain and their knights. But Ruon and Ildris were as close to true kin as Kallinvar had known since he was given the Sigil. They had been with him through everything.

"Brother-Captain." Concern painted Ildris's voice as they reached the middle of the walkway. It was littered with death, the bodies of Uraks, elves, giants, and men.

"We keep going. Pain is the path to strength." Kallinvar tried not to look down at the bodies. The dead on the ground did not bode well for what they might find within the chamber.

"Pain is the path to strength," the knights chorused, their armoured boots beating against the stone.

Great white banners marked with the symbol of The Order hung on either side of the council chamber's entrance. They billowed in the ferocious wind that battered at the tower. The enormous oak doors of the chamber were ajar; a dim light flickered from within.

Kallinvar steeled himself. He knew once he brought his knights through those doors, they might never walk out again. He reached out for his Soulblade. He did not summon it, but he wanted to feel it. To know it was there.

"Why fight me, Aeson? I don't want for madness and death. I want a world where we are not used as puppets by the Council. A world where we are not at the beck and call of lesser men. Alvira was my closest friend, but she could not see the truth. She was blinded by a misplaced sense of loyalty to an order that would have cast her aside without a second thought. I know you see past the lies. Don't throw away your life!"

Two men stood in the central atrium of the chamber. One was an elf with long white hair that fell over the front of his heavy, gold-trimmed, white-plate armour. Kallinvar recognised him as Eltoar Daethana, First Sword of The Order. They had met only once before. Eltoar loomed over the other man, a wicked greatsword clutched in his hands.

The other man was human. His studded black-leather armour was slick with water, and rain matted his short, black hair to his head. He held a sword in each hand, spinning them nonchalantly as the two men circled each other. A pair of dead bodies lay at their feet, both in the white-plate armour of the Highguard.

The central atrium was ringed by a colonnade of white stone, with statues of the six gods interspersed between them. Kallinvar's eyes fell on the statue of Achyron. *The Warrior. The duty of the strong is to protect the weak.*

A crack of lightning flashed to Kallinvar's left. About twenty feet behind the statue of Elyara, The Maiden, stood a gaping hole in the western wall of the chamber. Beyond the opening in the wall, streams of dragonfire roared through the sky, and the night was awash with a pinkish-black hue.

The two men did not notice the chamber's new entrants as they circled each other.

"You betrayed her."

"She left me no choice!"

"She trusted you, and you betrayed her!"

The man with the twin swords lunged at Eltoar, whirling his blades with incredible speed. He struck one out, testing his prey. Eltoar brought his greatsword up in time to block the strike, sweeping it back in a sideways arc. The other man – the one called Aeson – leapt backwards, just out of reach of the massive blade, and returned to circling Eltoar.

"You betrayed us all."

"Don't do this, Aeson. We do not have to fight each other."

As the two men circled each other, something caught Kallinvar's eye. Dark shapes hung in the air just below the golden dome. Bodies. *The council.*

Kallinvar took a step forward. "Eltoar Daethana. What is happening here?" The words resounded throughout the chamber, rising above the constant drum of rainfall on the golden-domed roof.

Both men stopped. Kallinvar imagined neither of them expected to see ten knights in full Sentinel armour standing at the entrance to the chamber.

An amused grin spread across Eltoar's face. "The Knights of Achyron? You have come out of your cave to save The Order? You are too late. Their *gods* did not save them. Achyron was nowhere to be seen."

Eltoar moved too fast for Kallinvar to react. The elf dropped his sword to the ground and stretched out his hand. As he did, an unseen force lifted one of the knights – Ohren – into the air and launched him towards Eltoar. In Eltoar's other hand, a níthral formed, an enormous greatsword wrought of shimmering blue light. He thrust the sword into the air, cutting straight through Ohren's sentinel armour, through his chest, and out the other side.

Kallinvar's heart lurched. A sharp vibration burst through his body from the Sigil fused to his chest. He felt Ohren's light go out. He felt his pain. He felt his soul scream.

To be killed by a Soulblade of any kind was to have your soul utterly destroyed. That is why the knights were given the Soulblades to fight the Bloodspawn: to ensure that creatures like the Fades could not return to the world. It was also why they refrained from using them whenever they could. It was a weight that rested heavy on a man's shoulders, to have ripped another's soul from the very fabric of the world.

Rage burned in Kallinvar. He had not even noticed he was charging, nor that his Soulblade was shimmering in his hands. The elf would pay for what he had done. He felt the power of the Sentinel armour coursing through him as he launched himself at Eltoar, the battlerush consuming him.

The air rippled with blue and green light as the two Soulblades collided. Kallinvar pulled back, pivoting on his foot, and struck at Eltoar's hip, only for the elf to block the strike in a flash of blue light.

Then, something crashed into Kallinvar's chest. It hit him with the force of a lightning bolt and sent him hurtling through the air. Kallinvar felt a crack as his body collided with something solid and a cloud of dust and stone consumed him. The Sentinel armour took the brunt of the blow, but his bones still ached, and he sensed a small crack in his plate, just below the breast.

Kallinvar's body screamed at him as he pulled himself to his feet. The other knights were charging at Eltoar, as was the man with the twin blades and black leather armour.

The elf just stood there, his hand outstretched in front of him. The sickly sensation of the Taint seeped into the air, oozing through it like a thick black oil. Panic set into Kallinvar's mind as he realized what the elf was doing. Using the base of the now crumpled statue that he had collided with for leverage, Kallinvar flung himself towards the elf. But he was too late.

He watched as Eltoar clenched his fist. All the knights and Aeson were stopped in their tracks and lifted into the air. Kallinvar was about five feet from Eltoar when the elf slammed his fist into the ground. A wave of concussive force rippled through the chamber, catapulting everyone in multiple directions. Kallinvar felt himself spinning again. He stopped only when he crashed into one of the columns that ringed the chamber. It didn't break, but he saw the crack that snaked its way through the stone. Once again, he dragged himself to his feet. He summoned his Soulblade and approached Eltoar.

Kallinvar watched as three of the knights, who were quicker to recover than he was, charged at Eltoar. He shuddered as they died. Two of them were killed by the elf's Soulblade, and the third was crushed inside his armour with blood magic. The Sigil pulsated as it flooded Kallinvar with loss.

He looked towards the statue of Achyron, then charged at Eltoar. *Pain is the path to strength.*

He gritted his teeth and let the power of the Sentinel armour flow through him. In seconds, he collided with

Eltoar. Flashes of green and blue light illuminated the chamber as they exchanged a flurry of blows. Kallinvar was a formidable warrior. He had fought enough battles to know this to be true. But Eltoar was the First Sword of the Draleid for a reason. And with blood magic flowing through him, he was faster and stronger than he had any right to be.

Every stroke of Eltoar's blade jarred Kallinvar's arms. But Kallinvar kept attacking. Out of the corner of his eye he caught a glint of steel as Aeson charged in behind Eltoar. The elf shrieked with pain as the metal tip of Aeson's sword pierced his left shoulder. Eltoar jerked forward, ripping himself free from the blade. He didn't have time to strike at Aeson though, as Ildris and Pirdin charged at him, their green Soulblades in hand. Within moments, the elf was surrounded. Ildris and Pirdin struck at him from the left while Kallinvar and Aeson moved in from the right. Ruon and the other three knights attacked fluidly, interchanging positions.

Eltoar took multiple wounds, but nothing seemed to slow him down. In all his centuries, Kallinvar had never seen someone fight as the elf did. He wielded his shimmering blue Soulblade as though he had been born with it in his hands.

A pulsating shiver emanated through Kallinvar as Eltoar drove the blade through Pirdin's heart. Another knight denied his rest in Achyron's halls as his soul was extinguished.

The sensation of blood magic touched the back of Kallinvar's mind once more as Eltoar sent another rippling shockwave through the chamber. It knocked Kallinvar back a few feet, but he kept his footing.

Loral, another knight, was not so lucky. She crashed to the ground and was consumed in a torrent of black fire that flowed from Eltoar's open hand. Her scream pierced the back of his mind.

Only five of them remained: Ildris, Ruon, Tarron, himself, and Aeson.

Bits of dust and stone plumed downward from the roof around the dome as a thunderous roar shook the chamber, followed by what sounded like a waterfall crashing against the dome above. Kallinvar pulled his eyes away from Eltoar as patches of the golden dome peeled away, glowing an incandescent orange. Globs of molten gold plummeted to the ground like drops of burning rain. Within seconds, an enormous hole formed at the centre of the giant dome. A large drop of the liquid metal slammed into one of Aeson's blades, knocking it from his hand.

Kallinvar saw only black through the gaping hole, where he should have seen the pinkish-red glow of the Blood Moon. Despite the new opening, the deluge of rainfall from outside had not filled the chamber.

His heart fell when two enormous, dark red eyes appeared in the blackness, like bonfires in the night. As Kallinvar's eyes adjusted, he saw that the hole in the dome was not filled with darkness at all. The flickering light from the candles illuminated a sweeping mass of overlapping black scales, accented with a light touch of crimson at their edges.

The enormous dragon craned its muscular, scale-covered neck through the gaping hole of the dome and into the chamber. It was the largest creature that Kallinvar had ever seen, though its true size was near impossible to determine as its scales blended into the night sky.

"Run!" Aeson roared. He took advantage of the momentary distraction to leap at Eltoar, driving his blade through the elf's ribs. "I said run!" he screamed again.

Aeson thrust his arm towards the sky. Arcs of blue lightning streaked from his fingertips, slamming into the dragon's face and neck. The dragon's roar sounded like thunder as it reared back out of the chamber. Aeson thrust his other hand towards Eltoar. The white stone beneath the elf's feet rippled like the surface of a lake, turning to liquid. It oozed up over Eltoar's feet, then up his leg, over his knee, locking him in place.

"Brother-Captain?" There was a mix of uncertainty and fear in Tarron's voice.

Kallinvar hesitated. "Go," he said, his feet already carrying him towards Aeson.

Eltoar had already broken free of his stone chains and was moving towards the young man, his enormous Soulblade casting a blue glow across the floor. Kallinvar leapt through the air, dropped his shoulder, and collided with the elf, sending them both tumbling to the ground. They were on their feet in seconds. Flashes of blue and green light burst through the air as they exchanged a flurry of quick strikes. The rain drummed against Kallinvar's armour as it fell through the now vacant hole in the roof.

He leapt out of the way as bolts of purple lightning shot from Eltoar's fingertips. The lightning streaked past Kallinvar and crashed into the statue of Neron that stood behind him, shattering it into a thousand pieces.

"You are becoming a nuisance." Eltoar stepped closer to Kallinvar, his eyes narrowed to thin slits.

Kallinvar did not respond. He just set his feet. Prepared himself. He let his chest expand, counting his heartbeats as he held air in his lungs, for just a moment. Eltoar charged, his shimmering Soulblade held high over his head.

Kallinvar released the breath he had been holding. He was ready to die.

Aeson stepped out in front of Kallinvar, blocking Eltoar's charge. Kallinvar could not sense the use of the Spark, but it was clear to him that Aeson had called upon it. The man threw out his hand and an ear-splitting noise like a resounding thunder-clap tore through the chamber, and Eltoar was ripped from his standing position. The elf careened through the air, smashing straight through the statue of Heraya and then further still, through the outer wall at the northern edge of the chamber.

"Run. We need to run, *now.*" Aeson stood at Kallinvar's side. His eyes were heavy and his breathing was laboured.

"But he—"

"He will be back, and so will Helios. If you want to live, we need to leave right now."

Kallinvar nodded. "Lead the way."

Rain continued to fall as they stepped out onto the stone walkway.

"Kallinvar. To me! The city is lost!" Across the gigantic stone walkway stood Grandmaster Verathin in his golden-trimmed Sentinel armour. Behind him was the Rift, a rippling pool of black liquid, with a pulsating green rim. The other knights must have already gone through.

Aeson and Kallinvar broke out into a sprint. They were about halfway to Verathin when a terrifyingly gigantic shadow swept over the ground in front of them. Kallinvar looked to the sky. An enormous black silhouette swept across the night, twisted, and dove straight for them. Just as a burning glow of orange flame flickered in the black dragon's mouth, it was struck by a bolt of blue lightning that shot from Aeson's fingertips. The dragon reeled away, disappearing into the night sky.

"Keep going!" Aeson shouted as they ran.

"You can't go through the Rift, Aeson. Not without Sentinel armour."

"Worry about yourself, knight. There are still things that need to be done here."

Helios's blood-chilling roar ripped through the sky. The immense beast had circled around the back of the council chamber and unleashed a river of orange-red dragonfire that crashed into the side of the stone walkway. The walkway shook violently as the section that was hit erupted in an explosion of stone and fire.

There was a moment where everything seemed to hang, suspended in time. Then, the bridge lurched. Kallinvar struggled to right himself as the massive stone bridge shifted, no longer able to support its own weight.

A thunderous roar informed him that the dragon had circled back around. The walkway shook again as it was struck by dragonfire. The section closest to the keep collapsed. Large pieces of stone tumbled down into the city below. The walkway had been separated from both the keep and the chamber. It now stood alone as its supports collapsed, teetering precariously.

"Go through the Rift, Kallinvar," Verathin said, as the two men reached the Grandmaster.

Kallinvar nodded, then turned to Aeson. "Where will you go?"

"Wherever I can survive. This fight is not over."

"You will always have sanctuary in the temple."

"For that, I thank you. Now go." Aeson turned away from Kallinvar before he had a chance to reply. The man stepped up onto the parapet and leapt off, down into the city below. Kallinvar had no doubt he would survive the fall. The Spark was capable of incredible things.

"We failed," Kallinvar said, turning to Verathin.

"No, brother. We have survived. Many of our brothers and sisters did not. This is only the beginning. We must rebuild."

"Ruon, Ildris, and Tarron?"

"Have already gone through."

Helios circled back around again. Kallinvar stepped into the Rift just as the walkway was bathed in one last breath of dragonfire. Blackness consumed him as he plunged into an icy well. He would live to fight again.

Pain is the path to strength.

DRAGONBOUND

The wind whipped around Coren's body as she pressed her armoured chest against Aldryn's scales, urging him onwards.

Flashes of pain burned through her mind like bolts of lightning. She could feel the long gash the other dragon had ripped through Aldryn's hind leg. She rested her hand against the dragon's neck. *Be strong. Now more than ever.*

A rumble of recognition from Aldryn touched the back of her mind.

All around them, the eldritch skies burned with rivers of dragonfire. The light of the Blood Moon caused the heavy black clouds to glow an incandescent pink, and the barrage of rainfall drummed against her armour. Everywhere her eyes turned, hulking silhouettes of dragons swooped through the sky above the city of Ilnaen, tearing each other to pieces. It was impossible to tell friend from foe.

It had all happened so fast.

A shiver ran up Coren's spine as a deafening roar pierced the tempest of rainfall and dragonfire. It came from above. She cast her eyes upward, her heart hammering against her ribs as she watched the enormous dragon burst from the dark storm clouds.

The massive creature careened towards them. It was easily twice Aldryn's size. A sea of overlapping dark green scales covered its body. The ridges of horns that framed its face were over a foot long, its neck was thick and muscular, and its yellow-orange eyes burned with a fury.

Coren and Aldryn moved as one. She let her mind slip into his and saw through his eyes as streaks of blue lightning tore through the night sky. The air rippled across their scales. Power coursed through their wings with every beat. There was no feeling like it in the world – two halves of one soul. To be Draleid. To be Dragonbound.

Aldryn wheeled out away from the incoming dragon, moving with such speed Coren would have been thrown from his back were it not for the intrinsic magic that held her in place, moulding his scales to her body.

Despite its gargantuan size, the creature turned with impossible speed, doubling back. Aldryn would not be able to get out of the way quickly enough. Coren needed to do something.

She reached out to the Spark; felt it floating in the back of her mind, a pulsating sphere of pure energy. The more she focused, the more she saw the separation of elements within the sphere. The five strands that twisted and turned around themselves.

Coren pulled threads of Water into herself, feeling their cool touch ripple through her skin and wrap around her bones. She weaved them into the deluge that fell from the clouds, forcing the droplets to coalesce into a sheet of water. Without missing a beat, she pulled on threads of Fire, using them to draw heat from the droplets, freezing them into a solid sheet of ice.

With a resounding crack, the green dragon crashed through the sheet of ice that hung in the air. A roar of confusion escaped its jaws.

Panic set into Coren's mind as the green dragon continued to hurtle towards them, disoriented and enraged, streams of fire flowing from the corners of its mouth. She could just about make out the shape of the Draleid who sat on its back. They were not large enough to be a Jotnar, and their armour shimmered with a golden gleam. An elf. Not that it mattered what race they were. Once they were bound, they were Draleid and nothing else.

Coren never thought she would see the day she rode into battle against one of her brothers or sisters.

"Draleid n'aldryr, Aldryn." The sound of Coren's voice was but a whisper against the crashing wind. But a rumble of recognition in the back of her mind let her know Aldryn could hear her. She pushed her body against Aldryn's scales, feeling their pulse slow to a steady beat. All panic yielded to an unwavering determination. They were ready to die, but they would take this traitor with them into the void.

A familiar pressure built at the back of her mind; an unstoppable, indescribable surge of power as Aldryn called forth his dragonfire. But in a moment, it was gone.

A series of flashes ripped through the sky in front of them, each one ending in a plume of gore and bloodmist that burst from the green dragon's body. One through the neck, one through the forelimb, and one through the chest.

A visceral roar resounded in Coren's eardrums as the gargantuan form of her master's dragon, Tinua, crashed into her attackers, burying his claws in the green dragon's side. Despite being twice Aldryn's size, the green dragon was but a plaything for Tinua, who towered over it. Tinua was one of the largest dragons in The Order, second only to Helios. His chest was deep, his limbs thick and powerful, his body armoured in crimson scales.

On his back stood Master Kollna. Her pale bluish skin gave off an odd shimmer in the eerie light of the blood moon. Her hand grasped a long spear of pulsating white light. A níthral.

With a flash, the spear soared through the air and caught the traitor Draleid in the chest, lifting them off the back of their now plummeting dragon. Coren felt a twinge of sorrow at the death of the dragon, and the Draleid. *This is not how it is meant to be. This is wrong.*

"Are you harmed?" Master Kollna shouted, interrupting Coren's melancholy. Her long black hair was tied in a knot and thin streams of blood trickled from various cuts along her face and arms. Not that they would slow her down. Not even in the slightest. Even for a Jotnar, Master Kollna seemed almost impervious to pain.

"I'm fine," Coren called back, weaving threads of Air and Spirit into her voice to carry it through the chaos to her master's ears. "What—"

"There is no time, young one. The city is lost. We must save the eggs in the hatcheries." Without another word,

Master Kollna and Tinua veered off towards the northern hatchery tower, one of three in the city.

A knot twisted in Coren's stomach as she urged Aldryn to follow Kollna and Tinua. She forced herself to look at the city below. The city that gave her a home when she had nothing. The city that turned her from a shipwrecked orphan to a Draleid.

Infernos blazed as far as her eyes could see, bathing Ilnaen in a maelstrom of orange-red flames that consumed everything they touched. Coren's heart twisted as bolts of lightning crashed down from the sky with such force that they tore buildings asunder. Even from where she sat, at the nape of Aldryn's neck, hundreds of feet above the tallest towers, Coren heard the screams of the dying as they were ripped from the world. A fury raged within her, battered by an unyielding wave of loss, and tempered by a numbness that sat like lead in her stomach.

She watched as two dragons fell from the sky, wreathed in plumes of fire and blood. Entangled in each other. They crashed through one of the city's sweeping arches and disappeared into the madness below.

"Don't look down," she heard her master's voice, augmented by threads of Air and Spirit, whisper in her ear. "You can't help them now. We need to focus."

Coren took a deep breath and steeled herself, letting her mind drift into Aldryn's. She would need to draw on the dragon's courage if she was going to make it through.

Just as Aldryn drew up beside Tinua, two massive dragons careened past, turned, and then spiralled back towards them in a terrifying display of agility.

Were it not for the calm that radiated from Aldryn, panic would have set its claws into Coren's bones. Instead, she reached for the Spark, drawing it into herself, pulling on threads of Fire and Air. She could not see her master's face, but Coren felt her reaching for the Spark as well. If they were not friends, she was ready.

The two dragons drew up on either side of Aldryn and Tinua. Both were larger than Aldryn, one a dusty brown, the other a dark ocean blue. Both were raked with claw and teeth marks from head to tail.

Coren held her breath as the groups flew side by side. The silence was so deafening, the rain hammering against her armour sounded like a war drum, calling her forth. *Please, be friends.*

"Master Kollna, by the gods it is good to see you!"

Relief flooded through Coren when she heard the words come from the Draleid on the back of the blue dragon and felt Master Kollna release her hold on the Spark.

"Master Dylain, son of Arin, it warms my heart that you are alive." There was as much warmth in Master Kollna's voice as Coren had ever heard. She had only met Master Dylain a handful of times, but she knew he and Master Kollna were close. "I wish we had more time. I need you to take Coren and head for the northern hatchery. I will make for the western hatchery. Above all else, we must save as many of the eggs as we can."

"It will be done, Master Kollna."

"Absolutely n—"

"We do not have the time to argue, young one," Master Kollna interrupted Coren, a gruff finality in her words. "Our duty, above all else, is to our soulkin."

A sense of pride radiated from Aldryn's mind into Coren's, at Master Kollna's words. *Draleid n'aldryr, Aldryn. My soul to yours.* She took a deep breath and nodded in acquiescence, more by instinct than anything else. Her master certainly would not have seen it.

"Coren, Farwen, with me. We must go now while the tower still stands." Without hesitation, Master Dylain and his blue dragon wheeled away, with the brown dragon following. Coren hesitated for a moment, Aldryn holding his position beside Master Kollna and Tinua. Some part of her knew she would never see her master again. It was just a feeling, but she knew it to be true. In an ocean of sorrow and loss, one more person should have been but a droplet – but it was more. Coren's heart ached; it pulled at her, commanding that she deny her master, that she refuse to be separated from her. But she ignored it, pushing its cries to the back of her mind. To be a Draleid was to feel more than your own pain.

As rain matted her hair to her face and the skies around her lit up with dragonfire, she stared across at the Jotnar who had found her that day on the beach, half-dead and coughing up water. Master Kollna was the closest thing she had to family.

"You are ready, young one." Threads of Air and Spirit carried her master's voice to Coren's ears. "You have a part to play in what is to come. Never forget, to be a Draleid is not simply a privilege. You must always rise, so that others rise with you. You must be the beacon they look to."

"Master Kol–"

"I am no longer your master. I am your sister. Draleid n'aldryr, Coren Valmar, daughter of the sea."

Coren fought against the tears forming in her eyes. "Draleid n'aldryr, Kollna, daughter of Luan."

With a roar, Aldryn pulled away, following after Dylain and Farwen. He shared her anguish. It peeled through the dragon's mind like rolling thunder. Coren pulled herself tight into his body, her fingers bunching into fists. *Dragonbound by fire, Kollna.*

Dylain and Farwen had almost reached the northern hatchery tower by the time she caught up to them.

"Dylain." Coren weaved threads of Spirit and Air into her words, bypassing the cacophony of death and destruction that rumbled through the city, sending her voice directly to the elf's ears. "What of the others? The Council? The Archon? What is happening?"

Dylain's response was short, and void of all hope. "Dead. I saw the Tower of Faith collapse with my own eyes, brought down beneath Helios's flames."

"Helios? That is not possible, Helios and Eltoar would never—"

"They would, and they did!" Coren had not heard Farwen speak until then. Her voice burned with loss and fury, as though everything she believed in had been ripped from beneath her.

Without another word, Farwen and her dragon veered off, diving towards the enormous tower of white stone that rose into the sky ahead of them.

"Much has been lost this day," Dylain said, a melancholy holding in his voice before his dragon dove after Farwen.

Aldryn did not need to be told to follow. But as they flew towards the tower, Coren caught a glint of something out of the corner of her eye. Something that tore through the sky at incredible speed. So dark were the dragon's scales that she would not have seen it were it not for the fire and lightning that illuminated the night. But she saw it, and it was headed straight for Farwen and Dylain.

"Go!" Coren pulled at the Spark as Aldryn shot towards the incoming dragon, drawing on threads of Fire and Spirit. The warm burning sensation tugged at the corners of her mind, as it always did when she drew on Fire. It was not a strand that she enjoyed pulling into herself, but it was effective.

The other dragon hadn't noticed them. It was too focused on Dylain and Farwen. That would give her a chance.

She held the threads of Fire and Spirit, pulling them in deeper than she ever had before. Then, in a flash of blinding light, she extended her hand out and unleashed a bolt of lightning so powerful it felt as though it was going to tear her arm off.

She watched as the lightning arced through the air, streaking towards the dark dragon and its Draleid. But then something happened that she could not explain. As if it had met with an invisible shield, the lightning crashed into something unseen and deflected into a nearby building, causing an explosion of dust and stone that plumed upward into the sky.

"What in the gods…" She had not felt the Draleid draw from the Spark. Even if she had, it would have taken immense power to deflect something like that. She didn't have time to figure out what had happened. The dragon would be on

Dylain and Farwen in a matter of seconds. *Take it out of the sky.* Aldryn gave a rumble of recognition, picking up speed.

A shudder ran through Coren's body as they collided with the other dragon. It shrieked as Aldryn caught its neck in his jaws. She felt the crack when his teeth broke through its scales. But at the same time the other dragon's spear-head-like tail raked a gash down Aldryn's side. The pain burned through Coren, as it did Aldryn.

A thread of Air crashed into Coren's chest, almost sending her plummeting into the city below. A flash, and a plume of fire shot from the dragon's back, just singing the edge of Coren's hair.

Trading whips of Fire and Air, and swipes of tooth and claw, they plummeted into the night.

Without warning, an earth-shattering tremor vibrated through Coren's bones and all sounds capitulated to a ringing that droned in her head as she was thrown from Aldryn's back. She tumbled across a hard surface before slamming into something solid. She coughed and spluttered, trying to loose the dust that had pulled its way into her lungs.

Dragging herself to her knees, Coren's immediate thoughts went to Aldryn, relief flooding through her when she sensed his heartbeat. She felt a few scrapes and cuts down his chest and neck, and the two gashes along his hind leg and his right side burned with a fury, but he was alive. A sharp pain just below her right breast let her know that she herself had broken a rib, maybe two. If the pain got too much, she would draw in threads of Spirit to hold it at bay.

Taking a deep breath, Coren looked at their surroundings. They had crashed into a building, that much was clear. But the foggy haze that clouded her vision made it nigh on impossible to tell which one.

She knelt there for a moment, her heavy breathing and Aldryn's heartbeat the only sounds that filled whatever chamber they had reduced to rubble. But soon, another sound echoed through the ruin: the wails of someone who had lost everything. Screeching, heart-rending wails so visceral and raw that Coren could feel the woman's anguish tearing through her.

Even then, in the chamber lit only by darkness and moonlight, before her eyes could focus on the scene in front of her, Coren knew what had happened. She felt it keenly, as though a blade had been dragged across her own heart.

A shiver ran up her spine at the mere idea of the loss the other Draleid felt. She did not want to see, yet she had to. She drew threads of Fire and Spirit into her eyes, calling on moonsight. The room lit up as though it were illuminated by a blazing sun, and her stomach turned at what she saw.

The body of the dark dragon lay crumpled in the rubble, the spear of a half-buried metal statue protruding from its neck. Coren's heart bled at the sight of it. She reached out her hand, resting it on the dark orange scales of Aldryn's neck. A sombre melancholy filled the dragon as they stood there, looking at the corpse of one that should have been his brother. Coren let her mind drift completely into Aldryn's. She needed to know he was there. To let him feel the comforting touch of her mind.

Following the blood-chilling wails, Coren's eyes fell on the woman who lay curled on the dragon's chest. Blood and dust matted her long blonde hair, and her body shook uncontrollably as she wept.

Coren swallowed the knot in her throat, then strode towards the weeping woman, her compassion dwindling with each step. *She brought this on herself. She betrayed her brothers and sisters. Betrayed The Order – the Draleid.*

"Why?" It was the only thing that Coren could bring herself to say. The only thing that made sense.

The woman lifted her head from the floor. Streaks ran the length of her face where the tears had worn away at the dirt and dust.

"Answer me!" Coren roared, a fury rising in her heart. She reached out to the Spark, pulling in threads of Earth. She dragged at the bits of broken stone that lay strewn around her, pulling them towards her, softening them, shaping them. Within moments, she held a long spear of white stone. It felt almost weightless in her hand. She wanted to drive it through the sobbing wretch's heart. "Answer me or I swear…"

"Do it!" the woman roared back. "Do it!"

Coren felt Aldryn tug at the corner of her mind. The anguish in his heart as he drew his snout up to the fallen dragon's face softened her fury.

"You brought him to this," Coren said, crouching down in front of the woman. "You were supposed to protect him. You were supposed to be his shield!" she felt her anger returning. "He died for you!"

The woman's sobbing stopped. She stared at Coren, her dark eyes gleaming in the night vision that moonsight provided. It was in those eyes that Coren saw it – the woman was broken. "I will not kill you. He died for you, but you do not deserve to die for him."

Coren released her grip on the stone spear, letting it shatter as it crashed to the ground. With that, she turned on her heels and made for the gaping hole they had created in the side of the chamber when they crashed through its walls.

"No!" the woman wailed after her. "Do not leave me like this. It's unbearable. He's not there anymore. I can't hear him… I can't feel him!"

Draleid n'aldryr, Rakina nai dauva. Dragonbound by fire, Broken by death.

"You made your choice," Coren whispered to herself as she strode away. The wailing stopped as she climbed up onto Aldryn's back. She knew what that meant, and despite herself she could not help but feel sympathy for the woman. The thought of losing Aldryn terrified her.

"To the hatchery tower, there is still more to do."

Aldryn rumbled in agreement as he shook the dust from his wings and lifted himself into the air.

Once they were free of the ruined chamber, it was only a few moments before they drew up on the northern hatchery tower. They had not been far from it when Coren had engaged the dark dragon. She spotted Farwen and Dylain's brown and blue dragons circling the outside of the tower.

"You can drop me at the main entrance and then join them. There isn't enough room inside for you to fight back if something goes wrong."

A deep growl sent vibrations up through Coren's legs as Aldryn voiced his disapproval. He did not need to speak for her to know his mind. Images of loss and pain flashed to the fore.

"I will be okay, you need to trust me."

The growl continued to resonate from the dragon's chest, but she felt his acceptance.

Each of the city's three hatchery towers stood at over five hundred feet tall and were more than a hundred feet in diameter. They rose above all else in the white stone city-scape, save the Tower of Faith.

The northern tower was the tallest among the three. Giant entrances were cut into its outer walls at intervals of fifty feet, with no entrance lower than a hundred feet off the ground. Coren narrowed in on the main entrance at the top of the tower. That was where Master Dylain and Farwen would be. She shifted in place as Aldryn drew closer to the enormous structure. Jumping from a height like this might have been safe with the Spark flowing through her, but that did not mean she found it any easier.

"Be safe," she whispered to Aldryn, launching herself from the dragon's back. The words were not loud enough for him to hear, but he did not need to hear her to know what she said.

Coren wrapped herself in threads of Air as she fell through the sky, slowing herself just a little as she drew closer to the top of the tower. She did not know what exactly she had hoped to see when she cast her eyes out over the burning city. Perhaps she had hoped it had all been a dream, but it had not. The Tower of Faith was a crumbled ruin, the western wall was consumed in a blazing inferno, and the rest of the city looked as though it had been under siege for a decade. Air whistled as it whipped past her face, holding back the sounds of roaring dragons and death. But in the raging tempest around her, she could see it for herself.

She dragged her eyes away from it all, struggling to suppress the sickly feeling in her stomach, and focused on what was below her. She pulled deeply at the Spark, pushing the threads of Air downward to blunt her landing.

With an audible crack, fissures spread through the stone beneath Coren's feet where she landed, plumes of dust and ash swirling up around her.

Rain drummed against the flat top of the tower, colouring the white stone a deep crimson with the blood it carried from the bodies that lay in crumpled heaps. Near all wore the white plate of the Highguard, the emblem of The Order adorning their chests. A quick look told Coren that Dylain and Farwen were not among them. So much death, and for what?

I'm going into the inner sanctum. Be careful.

A rumble of acknowledgment touched the back of her mind, along with the same feeling of worry that sat in the pit of her stomach. She pushed it down, swept her wet hair from off her face, and made for the staircase at the centre of the tower's roof.

More bodies lay sprawled at Coren's feet as she descended the staircase toward the inner sanctum. Were they good men who died defending the eggs? Or were they blood traitors who fell at Dylain and Farwen's hands? Did it even matter anymore?

The inner sanctum was the largest chamber in the hatchery tower. Its ceilings stood at nearly fifty feet, and almost all its diameter was open, uncluttered by supporting walls or colonnades. Set into the northern wall was an enormous archway that opened out into the skies, large enough for some of the younger dragons to come and watch over the eggs. It was a wonder of the craftsmages. Intricately crafted reliefs decorated the sanctum's sweeping ceiling, and rows of sconces cast warm candlelight across its length and breadth. Coren distinctly remembered the smell of burning wicks and suckling pork permeating the air.

But the inner sanctum was not as she remembered. The pungent tang of misery and loss crept into her nostrils as she stepped out of the stairway and into the wide-open chamber. The crashing howls of the wind, and the booming claps of thunder resounded through the chamber like the furious screams of the gods.

Bodies lay everywhere. Twisted, misshapen, torn limb from limb. Agony burned through Coren as her eyes caught the glint of candlelight against the shattered remains of eggshells scattered about the chamber floor. The sight of it took the air from her lungs and rent her heart.

"We are too late…" A solitary tear rolled down Coren's cheek, but she didn't move to stem its flow. There never would come a day when enough tears were shed for what had happened that night. The solitary tear turned to a river as an insurmountable wave of loss flooded through her mind. Her heart broke with the pain Aldryn felt, at the sheer despair that filled him. *There is more yet to do. Be strong. We will make them pay for this night, whomever is responsible.*

Even if she had not been Dragonbound, even if she could not feel Aldryn's heart, the visceral roar that poured forth from his jaws as he circled the tower would have told her everything she already knew.

With his loss, came her fury.

Reaching out to the Spark, Coren sprinted for the staircase that lay on the other side of the chamber. The misshapen corpses and the plate armour cut to ribbons could only mean that Uraks were already in the tower, possibly even the Bloodmarked. The drain had already begun to set into her bones, but she fought it. She would need every ounce of the Spark she could contain.

Shouts echoed up through the hallway at the bottom of the stairwell. The cries of men and elves mingled with the guttural howls of the Uraks. Coren pulled threads of Earth into herself as she leapt to the bottom, dropping into a roll as she hit the ground.

An Urak came charging at her before she could get to her feet, its leathery grey skin painted with fresh blood. With a howl, the creature swung its blackened blade in an arc. The gemstone set into the weapon's crossguard shone with a light as red as the beast's blood-chilling eyes.

Coren stumbled backwards in a desperate attempt to avoid being the next life claimed by the sword. Reaching out to the Spark, she funnelled threads of Earth into the floor below the Urak, pulling it apart to create an opening to the hallway below.

A look of surprise set into the beast's face as the ground disappeared beneath it. When its body was halfway through the opening, Coren brought the floor back together, dragging the stone to its original position, severing the beast's body at the navel. It howled as its legless torso crashed to the ground, blood and guts spilling over the previously white stone floor.

The Fall

Before Coren could get her bearings, another Urak crashed into her side, slamming her against the wall of the stone hallway. Panic set in as the creature wrapped its leathery fingers around her neck, the acrid smell of rotting flesh wafting from its open mouth. She grasped at threads of Air, tying them into a knot, pulling as hard as she could. Her body heaved with effort as she slammed the threads of Air into the creature, launching him across the wide-open hallway.

Coren did not release the threads of Air until she felt the Urak's bones give way with a series of snaps and cracks. She watched as the creature's lifeless body slipped to the ground, blood seeping from where its bones pierced the skin.

"Coren, down!"

Coren did not even look to see who had called to her. She felt someone draw on threads of Earth as she threw herself onto the ground. Seconds later, the limp body of an Urak dropped beside her, a long fragment of stone buried in its eye socket. Her heart pounded against her chest, like the sea in high storm attempting to crash through the hull of a ship.

She followed the sound of footsteps, to see an elf standing over her, arm extended. Three fresh cuts – claw marks, by the look of them – ran from the right side of the elf's jaw, down her neck, and over her now exposed collarbone. Her brown hair was cropped, with streaks of white dashed throughout. Coren had met Farwen but a handful of times. She had only become a Draleid a year or so before Coren. "What happened to you? we thought you were dead!"

"I ran into one of the traitors," Coren replied, taking Farwen's hand and pulling herself to her feet.

A grim look spread across Farwen's face. She did not ask any more questions; no answers were needed. Neither of them wanted to think about what was happening.

"Where is Dylain?" Coren asked. It felt strange not to refer to him by title.

Farwen held a knowing look in her eyes. "He's in the hatchery at the end of the hall, we… we were too late, Coren." Farwen's words caught in her throat, dolour filling her voice. "The Uraks, they… the eggs are destroyed."

"That can't… What about the other floors?"

Farwen shook her head, tears welling in her eyes. "They had already gone through the entire tower by the time we got here."

"There were hundreds of eggs in this tower…" A weightlessness took hold of Coren's stomach, and a wave of anguish flooded from Aldryn's mind into hers, consuming her every thought. His sense of loss was so raw that tears welled in Coren's eyes and streamed down her cheeks. Aldryn's heart felt as though it were a well of agony of which there was no bottom.

Coren held her breath in her chest, trembling as she released it. "Let's get Dylain," she said, wiping the tears from her cheeks, "there might be more in the other hatchery towers."

There had to be more. They could not have destroyed them all. It was not possible.

Coren's heart sank further as she stepped from the hallway into the hatchery. Only the slight flicker from the burning wicks of oil lamps broke the blanket of silence that dominated the air. The same heaviness of death held the hatchery in its grasp. Uraks, men, elves. Even the mangled remains of a Jotnar lay crumpled at the foot of one of the alcoves that lined the hatchery walls, it's pale bluish skin stained crimson.

Dylain sat on the floor at the other side of the room, his back against the wall and his arms rested across his knees. His sword lay on the floor beside him, wet with fresh blood.

"They're gone, and so is she," Dylain said, lifting his head, staring vacantly at Coren.

Coren paused for a moment, unsure what he meant. But then Dylain's words rang through her head – his dragon, Soria, was dead. In a panic, Coren reached out to Aldryn, feeling nothing but fury emanate from the dragon's mind. In the midst of her own despair over losing the eggs, she had not felt his emotions shift. She let her mind sink into his. Flashing images. Fire, claws, teeth. They were under attack. She watched as Dylain's dragon fell from the sky.

"Dylain, my heart mourns your loss."

The man did not respond. He did not so much as acknowledge that there was anyone else in the room.

Footsteps echoed through the hallway outside the chamber. Coren wove threads of Air and Spirit into her ears, amplifying the sounds. "At least fifty Uraks, probably more."

Dylain dragged himself to his feet, picking up his sword and using the pommel as leverage. Coren felt him pull on threads of Fire and Earth, far more than was safe. Without warning, he slammed the threads of Earth into the rear wall of the hatchery, sending an avalanche of stone tumbling down into the city below, and exposing the chamber to the pinkish light of the Blood Moon. "Go."

"What? Don't be an idiot," Farwen said, grabbing her master by the shoulder. "Enough has been lost today, we can't lose you too."

Dylain brought his free hand to his shoulder and placed it on top of Farwen's, giving her a weak smile. "I am already lost. I am not strong enough to join The Broken. But I will send as many of them to the void as I can before I follow Soria. Now go." Dylain gave Farwen one last look before approaching Coren.

"I…" Coren's words caught in her mouth.

"Keep her safe, Coren. Kollna has always spoken highly of you."

"You don't have to—"

"I pray you never understand why I have no choice. Not all have the strength to become Rakina. Some lose too much."

"May you find her again."

Dylain nodded, a glimmer of hope in his eyes. "Go, before you do not have a choice."

Coren turned towards the opening in the wall, looking out into the night. "Farwen, are you ready?"

The elf's gaze lingered on Dylain, as though she were contemplating staying with him. But after what felt like an eternity, she nodded.

Coren reached out to Aldryn. His mind was still ablaze with fury as he fought in the skies around the hatchery tower, but he heard her call.

"Farwen, we need to go now."

The elf gave another resigned nod, and moved to join Coren, but stopped halfway, turning towards her master. "Master Dylain."

Dylain turned to Farwen, his eyebrow raised.

"Die well."

A soft smile touched the edges of Dylain's mouth. "Live better."

With that, Farwen turned, sprinted towards the opening in the wall, and leapt out into the night. Coren thought she saw tears streaming down the elf's cheeks.

She looked at Dylain one last time before taking a deep breath and launching herself after Farwen. As she fell, Coren wrapped herself in threads of Air and reached out to Aldryn. Only a few moments passed before she felt the cool touch of his scales beneath her hands.

A rumble came from the dragon's chest as relief touched the back of Coren's mind.

"I am okay," she said, resting her hand on the side of Aldryn's neck. "We must not stop now."

A deep reverberation resonated from Aldryn's chest.

Coren wove threads of Air and Spirit into her voice. "Farwen, we make for the Eastern Tower."

THE TRAITOR

T he smell of rain and fresh blood hung in the air of the inner sanctum.

What had once been one of Eltoar's favourite places in the city was now nothing but a crumbled tomb. Less than half the sconces still held light, streams of blood incarnadined the white stone floor, and the chamber was littered with the bodies of those he had once called friends. The ceiling, that had once been so beautiful, was destroyed. The reliefs crafted into its alcoves lay in pieces.

But there was one thing above all else that set a pain in his heart: the shattered remains of countless dragon eggs that shimmered in the dim firelight. Fane had said they would be saved, but even he had no control over the Uraks – foul beasts. They served Efialtír and no one else. He had many names, The Traitor, the Blood God, the Harbinger of Shadow. But in the harsh tongue of the Uraks, he was 'Lifebringer'. Whatever his name, those beasts would die for him, and they would kill for him. Even the thought of calling those creatures 'allies' sickened him, but they were a means to an end.

Eltoar dropped down to one knee, picking up the broken fragments of a dull yellow egg. A snarl formed at the corner of his mouth, Helios's fury seeping into his mind. *I am sorry, old friend. This is not how it was meant to be.*

A dark resignation set into the dragon as he soared through the skies above the tower.

A new order. A world where the Draleid, and the mages, did not bow down to those who sought to control them. A world where the crown did not sit on the heads of simple people who sought nothing but their own gain. This was Fane's promise. Nothing worthwhile was ever achieved without sacrifice, Eltoar understood that, but this was not the sacrifice he had envisioned.

"I'm sorry." Eltoar rose to his full height, letting the egg fragment clink against the floor. His gaze lingered on the bodies that decorated the inner sanctum's floor as he crossed towards the stairwell on the far side. The creatures had been merciless. Even the stewards and servants lay lifeless, their bodies torn to pieces. Fane's words lingered in his mind. *'All those who do not join us, must die. It is a simple truth, Eltoar.'*

Eltoar understood the logic, but that did not mean that his heart was not torn asunder with the things that he had done. The image of Alvira's lifeless body flashed in his mind. He had held out hope, however small, that she might see the truth. Why could she not see? Why could she not see the hypocrisy of The Order? The fallacy of a system where those who held power were simply pawns to weak fools. He felt the anger bubbling inside him. Partly at her, but partly at himself, for failing her. He would mourn her death until time emptied the oceans and ground the mountains to dust. But now, he needed to focus. He needed to see if any eggs had survived the bloodlust of those vile creatures.

The bodies of two Uraks were splayed out on the ground at the bottom of the stairwell. Eltoar would not have even stopped to give them a second glance, were it not that one of them was sliced clean in half, its entrails spilled across the floor, and its legs nowhere in sight.

Before he could sate his curiosity, the sound of steel on steel, followed by crashing stone, drifted down the hallway. Eltoar looked once more at the severed torso of the Urak, pursed his lips together, and set off for the source of the sound.

As he ran, he reached for the sword strapped across his back, though all his fingers found was air. He had left it in the council chamber. The blade that took the life of Alvira Serris. In truth, it was not a weapon he ever wanted to hold again. Anger had consumed him in the council chamber. But after, as he sat astride Helios, and the rain drummed against his armour, slicking his hair to his head, the anguish had crept in.

Eltoar stopped at the entrance to the hatchery. A guttural howl came from within.

For a moment, he contemplated tapping into the gem-stone that hung on the chain around his neck, but only for a moment. Unlike the Spark, Blood magic – or the Essence, as Fane called it – did not draw its power from the soul of the wielder, but from the Essence harnessed from the souls of the dying. It was intoxicating. It did not dull or weaken you like the Spark, it flowed through you like a tidal wave of fire, igniting every aspect of who you were. Only the most powerful mages could harness and use blood Essence when it was first released from a person's soul. Eltoar had seen the life be burned from the eyes of weaker men who had attempted such a thing. The gemstone, however, acted as a buffer, storing the Essence and allowing it to be tapped into gradually. Eltoar pulled his hand to his white breastplate, hovering over where the gemstone was hidden beneath, glowing a dim red.

No. He would not use it unless he needed to.

With a heavy sigh, he shook the thought from his mind and instead reached out to the Spark, pulling on threads of Air and pushing them into the heavy wooden doors that guarded the hatchery. The doors gave way with ease, flying open into the enormous hatchery that had once been the pride of The Order in Ilnaen. Like the rest of the tower, it was nothing but a ruin now.

A gaping hole stood in the rear wall, opening out into the tempest that consumed the pinkish-black skies. All around the chamber, the alcoves that were set into the walls had collapsed in on themselves, crushing the eggs they had guarded.

At the centre of the room, one man in dark leather armour stood with his back to the opening, sword in hand. Blood flowed from a deep wound in his left shoulder, and his right eye was swollen shut. It took only a moment for Eltoar to recognize the man as Dylain.

Five Uraks stood in front of him, two were Bloodmarked. The hulking creatures dwarfed their smaller companions. They stood at least ten feet tall, weighed down with thick muscle that Eltoar knew belied a lightning-quick speed.

Blood rune markings covered their leathery grey skin, emitting an incandescent glow of red light and smoke. If battle did not kill them, the blood runes would. All blood magic required sacrifice.

With a howl, one of the Uraks leapt forward, swinging its blackened blade. Dylain sidestepped, sending the creature barrelling through a stone pedestal with a whip of Air. His success was short-lived though, as one of the Bloodmarked caught him with a vicious backhand that sent him spiralling to the ground.

Eltoar had always admired Dylain. The man was like Alvira, noble to a fault. It was ultimately a weakness, but an admirable one. The thought of watching such a man die at the hands of those creatures did not sit well with him. That was when Eltoar decided: pact, or no pact, these Uraks would die.

Reaching out to the Spark, Eltoar broke into a sprint. In the back of his mind, he pulled on each of the five elemental strands, drawing them into his body. A bright blue light shimmered against the white stone floor as his níthral took shape in his hands. Feeling the familiar power surge through his body, Eltoar bent at the knee and leapt into the air.

One of the Bloodmarked turned, catching sight of the blue light radiating from Eltoar's níthral, but the creature was too late. Grasping the hilt with both hands, Eltoar swung his níthral overhead, and brought it down in an arc over the creature's back. There was a momentary resistance, then the creature's leathery, rune-marked skin gave way. The beast let out a screeching howl, and its runes lit up with a flare of light as the blade sliced it in two from head to crotch. Dark red blood spilled over the floor, both halves of the monstrosity slopping to the ground.

Without stopping, Eltoar pulled on threads of Earth and one of the smaller Uraks screamed as the white floor turned to liquid and rose up around it swallowing it whole. The Uraks bones snapped and cracked as the liquid stone solidified once more, crushing the beast beneath.

Two more.

Eltoar swung his níthral in a sideways arc, catching the blackened blade of the Urak before it separated his head from his shoulders. He traded blows with the beast for a few moments before reaching out and pulling on two thin threads of Air. He slammed the two threads into either side of creature's neck. There was an audible crack as the beast dropped limp to the floor.

The smell of burning flesh drifted into Eltoar's nostrils. He turned to face the remaining Bloodmarked. Smoke plumed from the glowing red blood runes that decorated the creature's body.

The beast moved with incredible speed, reaching Eltoar before he could even think about swinging his níthral. Its enormous hands crashed into his breastplate, its claws burying into the steel, slicing through it as though it had been made of paper. In one motion, it lifted him off his feet, and slammed him back down into stone. Pain ripped through Eltoar's body.

Without releasing its grip on his breastplate, the beast swung its arm, launching Eltoar through a nearby pillar. As he lay there in the rubble, Eltoar placed his hand over his half-destroyed breastplate, hovering just above where the gemstone lay hidden. He held it there for a moment, before finally acquiescing. He tapped into the gemstone, and the blood Essence it held within. For a second, his vision went black, his skin cold as ice, and his body lost all feeling. But then the Essence flowed into him, flooding through his body, pulsing through his veins. Across the room, the Bloodmarked held Dylain's motionless body in the air, his enormous grey hand wrapped around the man's throat.

The power that pulsed through Eltoar's veins was intoxicating. He felt as though he could uproot mountains with nothing but a thought. There was not much Essence left in the stone, though. He would have to be quick. With the Essence surging through him, his legs carried him across the floor of the hatchery at a speed that should not have been possible. The Bloodmarked noticed Eltoar just in time to drop Dylain's limp body to the floor, and turn to face his attacker. The beast could sense Blood Magic; it could feel it at the core of its being.

Clasping both its hands together, the Bloodmarked brought them down in a hammer swing.

Were it not for the strength that flowed through him from the gemstone, Eltoar would never have seen the blow coming. But he did. He caught it with one hand, stopping the beast's downward momentum without breaking stride.

Even in the glow of the creature's eyes, Eltoar saw the surprise. He struck his free hand into the beast's chest, channelling the blood Essence into a ferocious shockwave. The Bloodmarked careened backwards, cracks spreading throughout the wall it collided with. Roaring with fury, it charged towards Eltoar.

Pulling the last of the Essence from the gemstone, Eltoar tethered the beast in place, its limbs stuck in position as though it were frozen in ice. Reaching to the Spark, Eltoar called on his níthral, driving the glowing blue blade up through the creature's sternum. He watched as the blood runes flickered as though trying to keep the beast alive before their light faded to nothing. With that, he released the creature's body from its tether and let it drop, limp, to the floor.

With the Uraks and the Bloodmarked sent to the void, the only sounds in the chamber were the constant drum of rainfall as it blew through the hole in the outer wall, and the deep, heavy breaths of a dying man.

Eltoar turned to find Dylain lying on his back, his head propped up against the base of a stone pedestal. Death would not wait long for him. The flow of blood from his shoulder was fatal by itself, but it looked as though the Bloodmarked had broken his leg and possibly some of his ribs.

Eltoar knelt down beside him, releasing his hold on the níthral.

Dylain squinted, as though there were a haze over his eyes. "Eltoar, is that you?" He coughed, his face twisting in pain. "What are you doing here? More will be coming, you need to go. Even you cannot fight them all."

Eltoar ignored Dylain's question, instead checking him over for more wounds. Not that there was anything he could do, he was no healer. "Can you stand? We need to get you out of here."

"Me? I am done. You know as well as I that I am not walking out of this tower." There was a brief pause and Dylain's eyes glassed over as he stared at something on the far wall, forlorn. "Soria is dead. One of the traitors murdered her."

A deep sadness seeped from Vyldrar's mind into Eltoar's. *Sacrifices must be made.* He told himself that over and over, but each time the words seemed harder to swallow. Would there be anything left of the man he was once this was all done? "I am sorry."

"Do not be sorry, my friend. Make them pay. Make them pay for everything they took from us."

"I…"

A look passed across Dylain's eyes when Eltoar hesitated. The man had always been sharper than most. He picked up on everything. "Why are you here, Eltoar?" He coughed again, a few speckles of blood dotting his lips, but his stare did not waver. "Why are you not by the Archon's side?"

Eltoar rose to his full height. He walked over towards the gaping hole in the outer wall, staring out over the burning city, out over the place that had been the only true home he had ever known. A nauseous feeling set itself in his stomach. He closed his eyes, letting out a soft, sorrowful sigh. Dylain was not long for this world, and the least Eltoar owed him was the truth, he could give him that. "Alvira is dead…"

"By the gods…" Dylain said, coughing as his lungs began to fail him.

"It was me."

"What do you mean? Eltoar surely…" Eltoar could hear the realisation in Dylain's voice. "How could you? You betrayed her, betrayed us!"

Eltoar felt rage bubbling. It was partly himself, partly Helios, and partly the lingering trace of blood Essence within him. Tapping into the gemstone and drawing on the essence always seemed to fuel that side of him. But he pushed it down, clenching his right hand into a ball. "I had no choice," Eltoar said, turning to Dylain, "She gave me no other—"

"You murdered those who called you friend. Slaughtered those who loved you. *You* killed Soria. It doesn't matter who swung the blade, her blood is on your hands!"

Eltoar felt Dylain reach for the Spark. Threads of Air wrapped around his arms and neck, pulling tighter and tighter. But the man was weak, Eltoar could feel him fading even then.

He pulled on threads of Air and Spirit, shearing through Dylain's threads with ease. Turning on his heels, he dropped to the ground in front of Dylain, grasping the man by his shoulders. His heart pounded and his hands shook. "How can you not see? We are not elves, humans, Jotnar… we are more. We are Draleid!"

"You are not a Draleid." Dylain all but spat the words at Eltoar. His voice oozed pure hatred.

Something inside Eltoar snapped. "And what are you?" he roared, unconsciously weaving threads of Spirit and Earth into himself, pounding his fist on the ground, sending fragments of broken stone shooting in all directions. "What are you without Soria? Are you a Draleid? You do not even have the strength to be Rakina – to be broken!"

Eltoar's chest rose and fell in heavy sweeps. He felt each beat of his heart as it pumped the blood through his veins. "Answer me!" he roared, pushing threads of Earth into Dylain. The man cried, howling in pain. "I said, answer me!" Eltoar drew deeper from the Spark, pushing harder.

He felt it calling him, urging him to draw deeper, to push harder. He answered its call.

"You…" Dylain said between short breaths. "Are not…" The man screamed as Eltoar pushed even harder. "You are not a Draleid!" he howled in defiance.

Eltoar shivered as the Spark surged through him. It filled him from head to toe. He kept pulling at it, pushing down harder. His veins burned and his soul cried out in pain, if he pulled any harder from the Spark it would burn him out, consume his soul. Dylain's bones snapped and cracked as his body gave way, yielding to Eltoar's power.

Eltoar relinquished his hold on the Spark, dropping to his knees in front of the crumpled mess of blood and bone that was Dylain's body.

For a moment, there was utter silence. The drumming of the rain melted into the back of Eltoar's mind, the battle cries that rang out through the city muted into a distant haze, and even Eltoar's own heartbeat felt as though it belonged to someone else entirely. He knelt there in the rubble of the hatchery, his gaze shifting between his outstretched hands and the mutilated body of the man he had once called friend. "I'm sorry," he whispered, tears forming in the corner of his eyes. Even then, he felt the lingering trace of the blood Essence stoking the fire within him, twisting his anguish into rage. He leaned into it, letting it take hold, anything was better than sorrow and loss. He slammed his fists against the floor, wrapped them in threads of Earth and Spirit, then slammed them down again. Eltoar roared as the tower shook and fragments broke off, falling to the city below. His roar was deep and primal, he felt it in his very core. Loss, sorrow, rage – then emptiness.

As he knelt there, an aching hollow in his chest, the walls of the tower shook again and Eltoar looked up to see Helios's head craning in through the opening in the hatchery wall, the night skies now obscured by a curtain of black scales. He felt the tower shift as it struggled under the weight of the enormous dragon who clung to its side.

Reaching up, Eltoar placed his hand at the end of Helios's snout, feeling the icy touch of his scales. Their minds were as one. Their heart ached.

All great things require sacrifice.

"We must go to him," Eltoar said, dragging himself to his feet.

Men scattered in all directions as Helios alighted on a cool patch of earth at the base of the Star Tower. Eltoar sat for a moment, at the nape of the dragon's neck. His throat was dry and a tremble still made its home in his hands. *It is for the greater good.*

He truly did believe in his cause. The Order was corrupt to its very core, Alvira could not see it, but he could. He saw how the Council twisted and manipulated, how they were beholden to the kings and queens of the lands, using the Draleid as their lapdogs. They had known nothing of honour, nothing of the things that bind the soul. But that did not make the things he had done any easier. Nor should it have. He would live with them until the day he was taken from the world. He had accepted that. With a heavy sigh Eltoar leapt from Helios's back, softening his landing with threads of Air.

"Commander." One of the men stood at attention before Eltoar. His voice trembled and his eyes flickered between Eltoar and Helios, eyeing the dragon askance. The man wore black leather armour with a red trim and what looked like a makeshift lion emblazoned across his cuirass. "He said to send you up as soon as you arrived."

Eltoar held the man's gaze. He tilted his head slightly. "Why do you fight?"

A confused look spread across the man's face. "For victory, Commander."

"No, *why* do you fight? Why do you stand here before me, watching Ilnaen burn. Why do you stand on this side of the walls, and not the other?"

"I… my family, Commander. They died in the siege of Antalar, during the Lyonin War."

"A war started by The Order," Eltoar said, shaking his head, "because King Alunil would not accept their laws… and because they wanted the gold in the Aonan mountains."

Eltoar remembered standing in the council chamber beside Alvira, both arguing against the council's decision to support Thrakia's war against Lyona. But their arguments fell on deaf ears, and The Order's coffers filled with Lyonin gold. Antellar was razed to the ground in retribution, to call it a siege was akin to calling a dragon a bird. Eltoar took a step closer to the man, never breaking eye contact. "And this is why you fight?"

"I fight to avenge them," the man said, standing a little straighter.

"You have your vengeance now," Eltoar said. "Will you continue to fight?"

"I will, Commander."

Eltoar nodded, pursing his lips. "I am sorry for your family, stay strong."

The Fall

Vengeance. It was as good a reason as any. Vengeance could stir a rebellion, push people to do things beyond what they ever thought they could. But could it support an empire?

The sound of Eltoar's footsteps echoed through the seemingly endless stone stairwell that led up to the top of the Sky Tower. Oil lamps sat in alcoves, set into the wall on the right hand side, but other than that, it was barren.

After what seemed like an eternity, Eltoar reached the top of the stairwell. He paused for only a moment. He knew what he would see when he stepped out onto the top of that tower.

"It is done?"

A man stood at the parapet looking out over the horizon where the dark of the night battled against the roaring flames of Ilnaen, plumes of fire streaking through the sky. His hood was drawn down over his shoulders and his black cloak fluttered in the wind. He stood no taller than six feet, with an average build. For all intents and purposes, there was nothing special about him. But Fane Mortem was the man who had brought The Order to its knees.

"It is done. The council are dead." Eltoar said, his thoughts threatening to swallow him whole as images of Alvira's lifeless body flashed across his eyes. Pushing them down, he stepped up beside Fane. "As is the Archon. The rest of the battle will not last long."

He couldn't take his eyes from Ilnaen in the distance. In truth, the point of no return had been reached a long time ago, but he had done terrible things this night. Things that would seep into his heart.

"We have done it," said Fane, turning towards Eltoar, his dark hair matted to his face from the rain that refused to take even a moment's respite.

"We have."

Fane leaned over, resting his elbows on the parapet, letting the rain drip from the ends of his hair. "Something bothers you, something besides Alvira."

The mention of Alvira's name sent a shiver through Eltoar's veins. Fane did not know her, not truly. He did not understand. Eltoar stood with his arms folded, took a deep breath, then let out a sigh. "I went to the northern hatchery tower." There was silence as the rain fell and the flames flickered in the distance. "The Uraks destroyed the eggs, Fane. Hundreds of dragon eggs… gone."

Fane stood back to his full height. He looked Eltoar in the eyes and grasped him by the shoulders. "Are our Draleid away from the city?"

Eltoar nodded. "They are."

"Well then, we will make them pay for destroying the eggs, my friend. Their usefulness has run its course either way. It is time I show you the true power of the Essence."

"But what of the pact?" Eltoar did not mention his own breaking of the pact, in the hatchery.

"They broke the pact when they destroyed those eggs. And in the new world, honour is currency."

Before Eltoar could say anything, Fane turned to look back out over the parapet. He pulled a satchel from beneath the front of his cloak, sliding his hands inside and producing an enormous gemstone that pulsated with a vivid red light. Eltoar recognized it immediately. It was a larger version of the gemstone that hung around his neck, hidden beneath his breastplate. A vessel of the Essence.

"Tonight, my friend, Efialtír grants us the power to hold sway over this world, to right the wrongs done to him by the false gods. For I am his herald, and the Blood Moon rules the sky."

Eltoar could feel the power radiating from the massive gemstone. It was like nothing he had ever encountered before. Even without attempting to draw from it, he felt its pull. Without warning the tower began to shake, a deep vibration resonating through the stone. All around them, the skies seemed to bend, as though yielding to the power within the stone.

"Fane, what is happening?"

"You are witnessing the true power of the Essence," Fane shouted, raising his voice above the thrum that filled the air. "You want revenge for what the Uraks did? You shall have it!"

A violent tremor ran under Eltoar's feet. He stumbled backwards as arcs of lightning shot from the skies around them, first one or two, then twenty, then hundreds, as though the gods themselves had unleashed their wrath on the world.

In the midst of it all, Fane stood, unmoving. His cloak billowed behind him, lifted by the ever-increasing fury of the surrounding storm.

"Today is the day The Order falls," Fane said, lifting the gemstone above his head, "and the rest of Epheria learns who we are."

Eltoar winced, raising his arm over his eyes as the horizon erupted in a flash of blinding light. He watched through squinted eyes as a maelstrom of flame consumed Ilnaen, bursting upwards before raging both west and east, touching the feet of the Lodhar Mountains and Mar Dorul. It was the single most devastating display of power he had ever laid eyes on. He watched as the city he called home for the past three hundred years was reduced to nothing but ash and bone, as everything that had defined him was stripped from existence.

He reached out to Helios, who stood at the foot of the tower, watching over the devastation that unfolded before them. He let their minds sink into one another. A torrent of emotion flooded into him. An almost indecipherable blend of man and dragon. Sadness, loss, anger, pride, fear. Everything was shared. Sadness at the sacrifices that were made. Loss of who they once were. Anger at the things that drove them to now. Pride for what they had accomplished. Fear that they had made the greatest mistake of their lives.

Images flashed through his mind. The eggs, Dylain, the lifeless bodies of the dragons and Draleid… Alvira.

He opened himself to the Essence within the stone and let it consume him, let it burn away his pain.

From the Author

Dear reader,

I sincerely hope you enjoyed *The Fall*. I am a world builder to my core. The world of *The Bound and The Broken* contains thousands of years of history, and it has been my pleasure to give you this little drop in the ocean.

As the series continues, I whole-heartedly intend on bringing you more novellas and short stories to bring you deeper and deeper into this world.

Thank you for trusting me with your time and your imagination – we have one hell of a journey ahead of us.

Always yours,

Ryan

GLOSSARY

Epheria (EH-fear-EE-ah): The continent of Epheria is one of the largest continents in the known worlds.

Ilnaen (Il-Nay-in): Elven city, home of The Order.

The Old Tongue

Draleid (Drah-laid): *Dragonbound.* Warriors whose souls were bonded to the dragons that hatched for them.

Rakina (Rah-KEEN-ah): *One who is broken,* or in the elven dialect – '*one who survived*'. When a dragon or their Draleid dies, the other earns the title of 'Rakina'.

N'aldryr (Nahl-DREAR): *By fire.*

Nai dauva (Nay D-ow-VA): *By death.*

Names

Alvira Serris (Al-VIE-rah Ser-is): The Archon of the Draleid.

Eltoar Daethana (El-twar DYE-tha-nah): The First Sword of the Draleid. Bound to the dragon Helios.

Kallinvar (Kall-IN-var): Brother Captain of The Second. Knight of Achyron.

Verathin (Ver-ah-thin): Leader of The First, Grandmaster of the Knights of Achyron.

Ruon (Rew-on): Knight of The Second. Knight of Achyron.

Ildris (Il-dris): Knight of The Second. Knight of Achyron.

Coren Valmar (Core-en Val-mar): A young Draleid bound to the dragon Aldryn.

Aldryn (All-DRIN): Dragon bound to Coren. Dark orange scales.

Kollna (Kol-nah): Draleid, master to Coren, bound to the dragon Tinua.

Tinua (Tin-ew-ah): Dragon bound to Kollna. Red scales.

Dylain (Dill-AYE-IN): Draleid, bound to the dragon Soria.

Achyron (Ack-er-on): The warrior god, or simply The Warrior.

Efialtír (Ef-EE-ahl-TIER): The traitor god. Efialtír betrayed the other six gods at the dawn of creation. He turned his back on their ways, claiming his power through offerings of blood.

Urak (UH-rak): Creatures whose way of life revolves around bloodshed. Little is known of them outside of battle, other than they serve the traitor god – Efialtír.

Jotnar (Jot-Nar): The Jotnar, known to humans as 'giants', are a race of people who have inhabited Epheria since the dawn of time. They are intrinsically magic, have bluish-white skin, and stand over eight feet tall.

Printed in Great Britain
by Amazon

50973583R00057